Cast of Characters

Melissa Gregory. A lowly anthropology instructor at Breckenbridge University. She just wants her office back.

Eric Trent. Also known as Handsome Lover Boy, he's a 26-year-old meteorologist who looks like a Greek god.

Professor Sley-Mynick. A nervous, rotund professor of biochemistry who's a refugee from Hungary.

Carstairs. An enormous fawn-colored Great Dane with an attitude. He disapproves of strong liquor and approves of pretty girls.

Doan. A small, plump, pleasant-looking private detective who "won" Carstairs in a crap game. He's bodyguarding Eric Trent.

Heloise of Hollywood. A 54-year-old cosmetics queen who still looks like a million bucks and is married to Eric Trent, who's half her age. Like several of the other characters, she has a secret past.

Beulah Porter Cowys. A middle-aged physics professor who's very protective of her friend Melissa.

Maximilian Morales. A janitor with eight children who claims to be a descendant of Emperor Maximilian of Mexico. But who is he really?

Frank Ames. A redhaired assistant professor of English who's sweet on Melissa. He's in the wrong place at the wrong time.

T. Ballard Bestwyck. The fearsome president of Breckenridge.

The Misses Aldrich. Elderly identical twins who walk, talk, and think in unison. They admire Carstairs.

Humphrey. A fat, pig-faced cop who hates Doan with a passion.

Shirley Parker. A pretty graduate student in psychology who's doing her dissertation on human sexualilty. Doan has his eye on her.

"Big Tub" Tremain. A carnival tough guy.

Books by Norbert Davis

The Carstairs & Doan trilogy
The Mouse in the Mountain (1943)
Sally's in the Alley (1943)
Oh, Murderer Mine (1946)

Murder Picks the Jury (1946)
as by Harrison Hunt,
written in collaboration with
W.T. Ballard

The Adventures of Max Latin (1988)
A Collection of Short Stories

Oh, Murderer Mine

A Carstairs & Doan Mystery

by

Norbert Davis

The Rue Morgue
Lyons / Boulder

Oh, Murderer Mine
was first published in 1946
New material copyright © 2003
by The Rue Morgue Press

ISBN: 0-915230-57-7

Printed by Johnson Printing
Boulder, Colorado

PRINTED IN THE UNITED STATES OF AMERICA

Norbert Davis

NORBERT DAVIS first introduced us to Doan, his private eye hero, in the 1943 novel *The Mouse in the Mountain* by saying he was "short and a little on the plump side, and he had a chubby, pink face and a smile as innocent and appealing as a baby's. He looked like a very nice, pleasant sort of person, and on rare occasions he was." He sounds like the typical hardboiled hero of the time, but readers back then were in for a surprise.

That surprise was his partner, a sidekick who bears little resemblance to the other private eye sidekicks of the era, such as Sam Spade's Miles Archer or Nero Wolfe's Archie Goodwin. His full name is Dougal's Laird Carstairs and he boasts a pedigree that puts Doan's to shame. A Great Dane, Carstairs is in a class all to himself in a long and illustrious succession of pets used in crime fiction, although we suspect Carstairs would tear your arm off if you called him a "pet." He certainly views himself as the dominant partner in the Carstairs and Doan Detective Agency, even though Doan "won" him in a crap game. Part of that dominance comes from his sheer size. Carstairs isn't just big. He is enormous. Davis describes him: "Standing on four legs, his back came up to Doan's chest. He never did tricks. He considered them beneath him. But had he ever done one that involved standing on his hind feet, his head would have hit a level far above Doan's. Carstairs was so big he could hardly be called a dog. He was a sort of new species." Doan also figures that Carstairs is his intellectual superior as well as being far better mannered. Boozing offends Carstairs, and Doan's frequent imbibing (from which he never shows any ill effect) always elicits a menacing growl, especially in the second book in the series, *Sally's in the Alley* (1943).

Hardboiled fiction was supposed to put the emphasis on action, and although you'll find plenty of that in Davis' books, his real forte was comedy. And Davis was at his comic best in the three novels and two short stories ("Cry Murder" and "Holocaust House") that showcased Doan and his remarkable sidekick. Modern private eye writer

Bill Pronzini said Davis "was one of the few writers to successfully blend the so-called hardboiled story with farcical humor." *Oh, Murderer Mine,* the third book in the trilogy, is easily the most farcical of his books and was published by Handi-Book Mysteries, a literary refuge for many of the low-rent private eye writers of the 1940s.

While the Doan and Carstairs canon make up three of only four books Davis published in his lifetime, he was an extremely prolific writer of short stories, although writing wasn't his first choice as a career. Born on April 18, 1909, in Morrison, Illinois, Davis moved with his family to California in the late 1920s, where he attended college, eventually earning a law degree from Stanford although he never bothered to take the bar exam. By the time he graduated he was an established pulp magazine writer. His stories were appearing in the leading pulps of the day, including *Dime Detective, Double Detective,* and *Detective Fiction Weekly* as well as *Black Mask.* Nor did he confine himself to crime fiction. He wrote whatever he could sell—adventure stories, love stories, westerns. In fact, one western story, "A Gunsmoke Case for Major Cain," was filmed in 1941 as *Hands Across the Rockies,* starring B western actor Wild Bill Elliot.

In his early years as a pulp writer, Davis was married to his first wife, Frances, and lived in Los Altos in the San Francisco Bay Area. After divorcing Frances, he married another writer, Nancy Kirkwood Crane, whose stories were appearing in such higher-paying slick magazines as *The Saturday Evening Post.* Davis himself began to make the switch from the pulps to the slicks in the mid-forties, selling a number of humorous short stories to them but never experiencing total success in this new medium. By the late 1940s, his stories were being rejected by some of the slicks while his wife's career was progressing at a rapid rate. In 1949, he and Nancy moved from California to Salisbury, Connecticut, perhaps to be closer to the New York publishing houses. That same summer, Davis drove to the resort community of Harwick, Massachusetts, on Cape Cod. There, early in the morning of July 28, he ran a hose from his car's exhaust to the bathroom of the house where he was staying. His body was discovered there later that day. He was just forty years old. He left no note. At probate, his estate was valued at less than five hundred dollars.

For more information on Davis see Tom & Enid Schantz' introduction to The Rue Morgue Press edition of *The Mouse in the Mountain,* published in 2001.

CHAPTER ONE

HERE IT WAS SPRING AGAIN, AND THE bees were buzz-
ing and the buds were bursting and the doves were cooing, and
the sun was beaming on all these and lots of other activities in a
benignly obscene way. It was just the same old tedious show that
has been playing return engagements at regular intervals for a
million years or more and certainly nothing to get worked up
over, but nevertheless it seemed new and splendid and fine to
Melissa Gregory, because she was happy. She was a simple and
uncomplicated sort of a person, and it didn't take much to put her
in that state.

She walked along the edge of the Old Quad now with her
head up and her shoulders back and her heels tapping in what she
considered a briskly competent manner. She was slim and tall
enough, and she had brown hair with copper-gold glints in it.
Her blue eyes tipped a little at the outer corners, and her nose had
three freckles on its bridge and turned up at the end. She was
wearing the wrong shade of lipstick.

She was being happy at this particular moment because she
had been promoted to a better job as the result of her outstanding
merit and her faithful record of attendance at faculty tea parties.

She was now an instructor. In the odd hierarchy of college faculties, an instructor rates somewhere between the head gardener and the lowest professor, if anyone can determine which one he is. An instructor is not allowed to lecture—or, for that matter, to talk loudly anywhere—but is entrusted with conveying the more elementary truths in certain subjects to beginning students.

Melissa taught anthropology, and she did this at an institution of higher learning called Breckenbridge University, Western Division, which specialized in the mass production of graduates of a standard size and competence. It was an efficient and impersonal sort of a place, but unfortunately one of its founders had once been on the campus of a well-known Eastern college and hadn't forgotten it. Consequently the campus of Breckenbridge had as much functional design as a bunch of dice dumped out of a hat. The buildings were scattered in all directions and hidden under ivy and behind bushes.

Melissa's headquarters was a building known as Old Chem because there were three beginning chemistry laboratories on the first floor. Old Chem was a solid, two-story, gray granite building with an ugly front and a splayed-out rear, and its architect had evidently had the theory that windows were designed to shoot Indians out of and not to facilitate the entrance of fresh air or light.

Melissa went up the block stone steps and through the arched entrance and then up the stairs to her right into the dimness of the upper corridor. Her office was the second one down, and she was fumbling in her purse for the key when she noticed that the door was slightly ajar. She pushed it open wider and looked in.

This was a fairly representative example of a college faculty office. It was quite a lot larger than a hall closet and ventilated about as well, and the furniture probably would have brought a comparatively good price at a fire sale. Melissa loved it in a proud and fiercely possessive way because it was the first one she had ever had that was hers and hers alone.

At present there was a man in it. He was sitting in Melissa's chair. He had papers spread messily all over Melissa's desk. And, in addition to all that, he was a young man.

Which was something to give Melissa pause, because when she thought about men—which was neither too often nor yet too infrequently—she thought about young men. As a matter of fact, when she was doing thinking of this sort and enjoying it most of all, she thought about a young man who looked almost exactly like this one.

Unfortunately, however, this was neither the time nor place for Melissa's dream-man-come-to-life to suddenly appear. Obviously, she couldn't go swooning at him even if she wanted to—and she told herself sternly she had no such desire—because he was an intruder. Worse than that, he had all the earmarks of being one of the vilest criminals the university faculty produced—an office snitcher—and here he was caught red-handed in an attempt to move into Melissa's quarters even before she'd had an opportunity to get settled herself.

"Well," said Melissa in a cutting way. "Good morning."

"Uh," said the young man. He was making some very involved mathematical computations on a scratch pad, and he didn't look up. "Uh," he said, and pulled a large, indistinct map toward him and made a careful, wavy line on it with India ink and a drawing pen. He was extremely handsome. He had blond hair that curled in ringlets and a straight, short nose. His eyes were blue, shaded with long, dark lashes. The effect of this collar-ad perfection was tainted a little by the way his mouth twisted down at one corner and the way he was scowling, but even at that he missed being pretty only by a very small margin.

Melissa stepped through the door. "I beg your pardon."

He looked up sideways at her. "What do you want?"

"Well, really," said Melissa. "It so happens that this is my office."

"Not any longer."

"What?" said Melissa blankly.

"It's mine now."

"What?" said Melissa.

The young man scowled. "Are you hard of hearing, or don't

you understand English? I'm going to use this office from now
on—exclusively."

Melissa swallowed hard. "Well, you can't just move in like
this!"

"I already have."

"Well, who gave you the authority to do it?"

"The president of the university."

"Oh," said Melissa.

The young man eyed her coldly. "Was there anything else?"

Melissa's voice was shaky. "But—but all my files and notes
are in here."

"Not now, they aren't," said the young man. He pulled one
of the desk drawers open to illustrate that it was empty.

"My files!" Melissa shrilled. "My class notes! What have
you done—"

"Nothing," the young man said shortly. "I didn't touch them.
Some dusty, beefy party who makes noises like a tin mouse took
them away."

"Do you mean Professor Sley-Mynick?"

The young man shrugged. He had custom-built shoulders.

Melissa took a deep breath. "Now look here, this is all wrong,
and I don't care what the president of the university said. This
office is mine. It was assigned to me. You haven't any right to
just walk in and take it."

"What's your subject?" the young man asked indifferently.

"Anthropology."

"Oh, that silly stuff. You don't need any particular office for
that. Go find one somewhere else."

Melissa swallowed again. "What is your subject?"

"Meteorology."

"Hmmph," said Melissa contemptuously. "And just why do
you need this particular office for that?"

The young man jerked his thumb toward the ceiling. "It has a
trap door. My instruments are on the roof."

"What instruments?" Melissa asked. "I thought you people
used crystal balls to predict the weather."

The young man didn't answer. He just curled his lip. He reached down and rattled the weather map. He was waiting very pointedly for Melissa to leave.

Melissa changed her tactics. "Now, listen," she said, smiling. "I really want this office. This particular one. I like it. And I was here first. Let's make a deal."

"Let's not."

Melissa lost her smile. "Well, damn you anyway, you supercilious imitation of a Greek statue. This office is the only one in the building that has a private ladies' powder room. Do you think I'm going to come here and knock on the door and ask your permission every time I—well, every time?"

"I know you're not. I have to make progressive calculations, and it's important that I'm not interrupted in the middle of them when I'm plotting a front. You'll have to make some other arrangements."

Melissa breathed hard through her nose, staring at him. He stared back.

"I've seen you somewhere before!" Melissa stated accusingly.

To her amazement, he cringed. There was no other word for it. Melissa watched him narrowly, sensing her advantage, but not knowing what it was.

"Yes," she said, feeling her way. "I *know* I've seen you somewhere before. Your face is very familiar."

He was blushing, very painfully. The flush crawled in red waves up from his collar.

"What's your name?" Melissa demanded.

He moistened his lips. "Eric Trent."

It didn't mean a thing to Melissa. She was baffled.

Eric Trent knew it, and he sighed lengthily. "If you don't mind, I'd like to get on with my work. Good day."

Melissa scrambled around frantically in her mind looking for an inspiration. She didn't find one. "Oh, all right." She shot her hand out suddenly, forefinger pointed rigidly. "But I'll remember where I've seen you! And then, you'll find out!"

She stepped back into the hall and slammed the door violently, and then she marched down the stairs and back along the lower hall to the office door opposite the largest of the chemistry labs. She hammered on the dark, scarred panels vigorously. There was no answer. Impatiently Melissa tried the latch. It clicked, and she pushed the door open and looked in the office. It was larger and considerably more cluttered than hers, and dust motes stirred and glinted uneasily in the sun beams that pried their way through the narrow windows. There was no one in sight.

Melissa shut the door, and then she had a sudden hunch and opened it again very quickly. She caught Professor Sley-Mynick in the act of crawling cautiously out from under his desk. He froze there on his hands and knees and made wordless little pip pipping noises.

Also, he seemed to be stuck, for he was by no means a small man and the space he was in looked to be about three sizes too small. He was fat, as a matter of fact—fish white and jelly fat— but despite his size, the fierce, jet-black mustache he was wear- ing was still too big for him and Melissa got the impression the mustache was leading him around willy-nilly. He was bald and wore tiny rimless spectacles so thick they were opaque.

"Good morning, Professor," Melissa said.

"Oh," said Professor Sley-Mynick. "Yes, it is. Good, I mean. Isn't it?"

It was strange hearing such a pipsqueak voice emerge from such a roly-poly body. By dint of great exertion, the professor extricated himself from the trap he was in.

"What were you doing under your desk?" Melissa asked.

"Desk?" Professor Sley-Mynick repeated blankly. He spoke with an accent that gave his words a just noticeable blubber. "Under it? Oh. My fountain pen. I mean, it dropped and rolled, I guess. Didn't it?"

"No," said Melissa. "It didn't. You were hiding."

"I?" said Professor Sley-Mynick, amazed.

"Yes, you."

"From—from what?"

"Me."

"Why?"

"Because you are the senior professor in this building, and you are in charge of assigning offices in it!"

"Oh, dear," said Professor Sley-Mynick.

"Just what," said Melissa, "do you mean by giving my office to that matinee-faced moron upstairs?"

"Oh, he's not a moron. He's a meteorologist. It's the science of the weather—storms and the climate and—and things. It's very important work. He said."

"Never mind what he said. Answer my question. Why did you give him my office?"

"Oh, that," said Professor Sley-Mynick. "The president! T. Ballard Bestwyck. He's the president of the whole university. He talks to rich people—face to face—and they often give him some of their money. That's very vital. He wrote a letter. To me—personally. It said that the moron—I mean, the meteorologist—was to have an office in this building. I'll find it. The letter. It's right here. Isn't it?" He burrowed busily among the papers on his desk.

"I don't care about the letter," Melissa told him. "Why did you have to give this seasonal swami my office?"

"He said he wanted it."

"Oh, he did? And that was reason enough?"

"Yes," Professor Sley-Mynick admitted. "I mean, he's a very handsome young man, but I'm afraid he's not very nice. He snarls. Doesn't he?"

"Yes," said Melissa, sighing. "All right, Professor. Have you given any thought to finding another office for me?"

"Indeed, yes!" said Sley-Mynick. "Number 5. All your files and notes are in there. I was very careful of them. You'll like Number 5. It's nice. Isn't it?"

"It most certainly is not! It stinks!"

Melissa was speaking the literal truth. Number 5 occupied an unused corner of one of the chemical labs, and its partitions were porous. It is a moot question whether students like to make stinks because they take chemistry or whether they take chemistry because they like to make stinks. In any event, they invariably do.

"It's not right," said Melissa. "The whole thing is nothing but an injustice. You know that, don't you?"

"Oh, dear," said Professor Sley-Mynick.

"And do you know what I'm going to do one of these fine days?"

"What?" Professor Sley-Mynick asked.

"I'm going to spit right in one of his beautiful eyes!"

"Oh!" said Professor Sley-Mynick, deeply shocked.

Melissa slammed his door and started down the hall in the general direction of Number 5. She had gone about ten paces when something stirred sluggishly in the shadows. Melissa stopped with a startled gasp. It was too early yet for students to be lurking about, and anyway this couldn't possibly be mistaken for one.

It was a dog. It was the most enormous dog Melissa had ever seen. It sat right down in the hall in front of her in a leisurely and self-possessed way and proceeded to look her over from head to foot in a manner that was not far from insulting.

Melissa caught her breath. "H-hello," she said timidly. She snapped her fingers in a feeble attempt at friendliness.

The dog studied her fingers as though he had never seen any before and wouldn't care if he never did again. He was a fawn-colored Great Dane.

"Hello," said a voice.

Melissa jerked around. There was a man leaning against the wall, watching her. He hadn't been there two seconds before. He was small and plump and pleasant-looking. He was wearing a double-breasted pin-striped blue suit with outsize lapels and a dark blue hat. He had a naively appealing smile and a smooth, roundly pink face. He moved his head to indicate the dog and said:

"I use him for a decoy. While people gape at him, I sneak up behind them and pinch them."

"P-pinch them?" Melissa repeated, shying away.

"A slang expression," the man explained. "I mean, I arrest

them. I'm a detective. What are you?"

"An anthropologist."

"Oh," said the man. "You study apes and like that?"

"No! Certainly not! Anthropology is the study of mankind. We study apes only because you can learn a lot about men from them."

"I'll bet that's the truth," said the man. "My name is Doan. What's your name?"

"Melissa Gregory."

"Hello," said Doan. "That's Carstairs in front of you. He works with me—that is, when he's not working against me or just not working."

"He looks like a very good dog."

"That's what he looks like," Doan agreed. "I've got a word of warning for you."

"A what?" Melissa asked, staring at him.

"A word to the wise. Lay off the bird in your office. He's not for sale or for rent."

"What?" said Melissa.

"Eric Trent," Doan explained. "Mustn't touch."

"What?" said Melissa.

Doan sighed. "You must not make passes at Eric Trent. That is verboten."

Melissa's eyes narrowed. "I don't believe I like the idea you're selling. Suppose you elaborate on it "

"It's simple," Doan told her. "I keep females from making love to Eric Trent."

"Well, why?"

"Because I've been hired to do it. And, believe me, it's a full-time job. Women fall for him in squads. I mean, they would fall—over backwards—if I didn't stop them."

"I understand the words you're saying," Melissa said. "But they don't seem to make sense. Are you seriously telling me that this—this person has a bodyguard to keep women from falling to love with him?"

"That's right," Doan agreed. "And I'm it."

Melissa shook her head groggily. "Well, why? I mean, I'll agree, just for the sake of argument, that there might be one or two women in the world hard up enough or dumb enough to want that insolent imbecile, but they're the type who would deserve him if they got him. Why should either he or you worry about them?"

"We're not," said Doan. "But his wife is."

"Oh. He's married?"

"And how."

"Hmmm," said Melissa. "Now wait a minute. I'm just catching up with you. You have the barefaced insolence to warn me. I think I'll slap your face."

"Don't," Doan warned. "Carstairs will bite you if you do. Not that he cares anything about me, but he would feel it was a reflection on him."

Melissa looked at Carstairs. He was lying down on the floor with his eyes shut.

"Don't let him fool you," said Doan. "He's ready to go into instant action. He's just pretending he's not interested."

"Hmmm," said Melissa. "You know, this is all sort of fascinating in a repugnant way, and I know I've seen this Trent party before, but I can't remember where. Have you any idea where I could have seen him?"

"Yes," said Doan.

"Well, where?"

"His wife is Heloise of Hollywood."

"Heloise," Melissa repeated. "Of Hollywood. Oh!"

"Oh," Doan agreed.

"Now wait," said Melissa. "Now wait a minute. . .I know! He's Handsome Lover Boy!"

"Yup," said Doan.

"Stay right here!" Melissa ordered. "I'll be right, back?"

She ran down the hall and through the malodorous gloom of the chem lab. The door of Number 5 was open, and her notes were arranged in well-ordered confusion all over the floor and the swaybacked desk. Melissa dug through them, spewing lecture fragments in all directions, until she found the current issue of a large and slick and all too popular woman's magazine. She trotted back to the hall, thumbing eagerly through the back pages of the magazine.

"Wait, now," she said. "I know I saw one. . .Here!"

It was a full-page ad. In the upper left-hand corner there was a portrait photograph of a very handsome young man in a naval officer's dress whites. The very handsome young man was Eric Trent. Under it there was a message in artistically slanted and swirly facsimile handwriting.

> " . . and I can hardly bear the thought of the endless, weary days that must somehow pass before I can find safe haven once more in the dear circle of your strong arms . . but I too know my duty, dear one. . . and I shall keep alive the beauty that charmed you . . . keep it alive and glowing until your return, my own handsome lover boy. . ."

"Doesn't that make you feel like you just picked up a dead fish?" Melissa asked.

"Sort of," Doan agreed.

"I thought it was just an advertising gag," Melissa said. "I had no idea that anyone in the world would have a strong enough stomach to aim drool like that at an actual person and do it in public. Is this really a picture of Heloise of Hollywood, too?"

"Oh, yes," said Doan.

A second portrait, three times the size of Eric Trent's, filled up the lower right of the ad. This was a woman. It was taken in profile, and she had her head tilted back to show the long, smooth line of her throat. She had blond hair, and a cold, smooth, ice-frosted beauty. She looked as artificial, but just as well-designed, as a wax orchid. There was a message beside her picture, too, but this one was in printing, not in handwriting.

> ". . .Heloise of Hollywood, fifty-four years young, at

the supreme pinnacle of gracious, mature beauty—poised, assured, alluring—waits with calm confidence for the return of her own young hero-husband. Heloise of Hollywood has the glamour that is the rightful and easily obtained heritage of the Woman-Over-Forty. Heloise of Hollywood Beauty Prescriptions, compounded exclusively for the mature woman, are on sale at all the really discriminating shops from coast to coast. . ."

Melissa tilted her head judicially. "Fifty-four? And she looks like this?"

"Well, pretty near," Doan said.

"And she hired you to watch her husband?"

"Yes," Doan agreed.

"I still want to know why. It doesn't sound reasonable. It isn't the sort of thing a normal person would do."

Doan shrugged. "I'm just a hired hand, myself."

Melissa watched him curiously. "Well, what is Trent doing here? That nauseating junk Heloise of Hollywood peddles is piled neck-deep in every department store in the country, and it's expensive. She must make millions, and I've got a good idea what Trent's salary is. Did she throw him out?"

"No," said Doan.

"Oh-ho!" said Melissa suddenly. "Now I get it? He walked out on her, didn't he?"

"No," said Doan flatly.

"He did, too! That explains everything." Melissa tapped the magazine. "She has run hundreds of these ads in all the big women's magazines in the last couple of years. Every one of them had a picture of and some sort of a sticky message to Handsome Lover Boy. She must have spent millions of dollars promoting that angle."

"I wouldn't know," said Doan.

"Oh, yes you would. The whole point of that campaign was and is that if you're anywhere under ninety years old and use her stuff, you'll make yourself irresistible to men—just like *she* is!

Yes, and you can catch yourself a handsome young husband, just like *she* did!"

"You're probably wrong," said Doan.

"I am not. And now he's walked out on her in spite of all her mature allure. *Oh-ho!* And now her pretty pretty advertising campaign is about to backfire right in her face! No wonder she hired you to keep women away from him. If he falls for some twenty-year-old twirp and starts a divorce action in all the headlines, she wouldn't be able to sell that stuff of hers for axle grease."

"Have you ever heard of something called slander?" Doan inquired.

"Hmmph," said Melissa. "That doesn't prevent me from laughing at him and at her, too. And that's just what I'm doing. Ha-ha-ha-ha! I'm just practicing now, waiting for the next time I see that gloomy gigolo upstairs."

"What's the joke?" a voice asked. Its owner was a woman. She had sleek, carefully groomed gray hair, cut short, and she wore a tailored blue suit. Her face slanted from above and from below, culminating in a beak of a nose that made her look like an intelligent and slightly sinister eagle in search of a free meal.

"Oh, hello," said Melissa. "This is Mr. Doan. This is Beulah Porter Cowys, Mr. Doan."

"Hello," said Beulah Porter Cowys to Doan. "What do you do? You look too stupid to be a student, if you'll pardon me for mentioning it."

"Quite all right," said Doan. "You're being deceived by my detecting expression. I put it on to fool desperate criminals. I'm actually very clever, indeed. In fact, many people, including me, think I'm the smartest detective in the world."

"A detective," said Beulah Porter Cowys. "Now I've seen— What on earth is that?"

"A dog," Doan told her.

"Is he dead?"

"No. Just bored."

"His name is Carstairs," Melissa volunteered.

"Gaaah," said Beulah Porter Cowys. "It would be. I hate dogs."

"That's all right," said Doan. "He hates people."

"Was he what you were laughing at?" Beulah Porter Cowys asked Melissa.

"No," said Melissa. "Look, Beulah. See this picture? Handsome Lover Boy? He's upstairs."

"What?"

"It's a fact," Melissa told her. "Really. He actually exists, and he's really married to this Heloise. He's a meteorologist, or so he claims. Isn't it horrible?"

"Isn't what horrible

"Why, she must be almost twice his age."

"Just twice," Doan said. "He's twenty-six."

"Ugh!" said Melissa.

"Melissa," Beulah Porter Cowys said, "did you ever try stopping to think before you started talking?"

"What?"

"It just so happens that I admit to being forty-nine, myself. What's so repulsive about that?"

"Oh!" said Melissa. "Well—well—well, you don't keep a gigolo."

"That's because I can't afford one."

"Oh now, Beulah," said Melissa. "You're just saying that. What I meant was that it's sort of ugly to think about old people having—having—well, having ideas."

"There are some aged male movie comedians who don't seem to agree with you."

"Oh, them," said Melissa. "They're just sexual neurotics. It's a transference of the youth-longing. Shirley Parker explained it all to me. It's the same sort of urge that makes nasty old men peep into grade-school girls' playgrounds."

"That Shirley Parker," said Beulah Porter Cowys. "She can always give me the creeps in five seconds flat. She makes life sound like an unsupervised pigsty. She and her Freudian theories of motive analysis are enough to turn anyone's stomach. But what I want to know right now is, why is this alleged detective hanging around here?"

"Beulah," said Melissa, "that's simply priceless."

"Remember what I said about slander," Doan warned.

"Pooh! Beulah, this old hag—Heloise, I mean—hired him to keep women away from her pretty husband. I mean, actually. Isn't that a scream?"

"Oh, I don't know," said Beulah Porter Cowys. "Knowing what I know about the morals of the younger generation—and do I know!—I think it's a good idea."

"Oh, Beulah! You're just pretending—"

Something dropped and made a tinny battering clatter inside the second chem lab.

"It's that damned janitor eavesdropping again!" Beulah Porter Cowys snapped angrily. "Morales! Come here!"

A man eased himself out of the lab and looked at them in an elaborately surprised way. He was short and solid and lackadaisically stoop-shouldered, and he made each move as though it were the last allowed him and he intended to draw the process out as far as possible. He wore a battered black hat and a shirt with strategic holes in it and overalls that bagged improbably in the rear. He was carrying three galvanized pails in one hand and a floor brush over his shoulder.

"Hallo, peoples," he said in a liquidly lazy way. "You want something of Maximilian Morales, no?"

"No," Beulah Porter Cowys agreed. "Go away somewhere."

"Wait a minute," Melissa intervened. "Morales, can't you do something about the smell in Number 5?"

"I?" said Morales. "No."

"Yes, you can. You can calcimine those partitions or something—at least, that'll give the place a new kind of an odor."

"Calcimine?" said Morales. "I? I have eight children, señorita."

"What has that got to do with it?"

"Señorita, it is very hard to have eight children. It makes a man tired. I, Maximilian Morales, am tired."

"Well, stop having children then."

"Señorita, you are unreasonable."

"Eight children are enough."

"No," said Morales. "You will pardon me, señorita, but eight children are not enough."

"Why not?"

"Because none of them are any good. That is why it is necessary for me to arrange to have a ninth. Perhaps it will be smart enough to provide a comfortable old age for its honored father and jobs for its stupid brothers and sisters. One can only hope and keep trying."

"For how long?" Beulah Porter Cowys inquired.

Morales shrugged wearily. "That, of course, becomes a question one often considers at our age."

"Just be careful, now, Morales," Beulah Porter Cowys warned.

"I am always careful, señorita. It becomes an established mannerism in one of my breeding. You have, no doubt, heard of my great-great-great grandmother?"

"Too many times."

Morales nodded politely at Doan. "My great-great-great grandmother was regarded with a certain amount of favor by the great Maximilian, Emperor of all Mexico."

"Congratulations," Doan said.

"Thank you, señor. Is that your dog lying on the floor which is my care and responsibility?"

"Yes."

"Has the dog been trained, señor, to avoid—ah—accidents of an intimate nature?"

"He's very well educated," Doan said.

"You relieve my mind, señor. It is easy to see that with a dog of such great stature, an accident might be overwhelming."

"He never slips."

"He is to be congratulated. Now, if you will excuse me, I will resume my duties."

"Here," said Melissa. "Wait a minute. Aren't you going to do anything about fixing up Number 5?"

"Naturally not," said Morales, disappearing into the lab.

"Why all this sudden concern about Number 5?" Beulah Porter Cowys asked.

"Handsome Lover Boy has appropriated my office."

"Well, didn't you remonstrate with him?"

"Certainly. He just sat and sneered."

"Did you kick to Sley-Mynick?"

Melissa shrugged. "Yes, but you know how he is. Handsome Lover Boy evidently sneered at him, too, and that threw him into an outside loop."

"Is Sley-Mynick the puffy guy who pip-pips at people?" Doan asked. "What goes with him, anyway? He acts like someone had just given him a hotfoot."

"He's troubled with international spies," Beulah Porter Cowys said.

"Beulah," said Melissa, "it's not really right to make fun of him. He's a refugee, Mr. Doan. He's a very brilliant research biochemist. He was a professor at some university near Budapest with a name I can't pronounce. I don't know just what he did, if anything, but when Hungary threw in with Hitler, Sley-Mynick was arrested and put into a concentration camp. They must have treated him terribly there. Apparently it wrecked his nervous system."

"Did he escape from the place?" Doan asked.

"No. They decided, after they had half-killed him, that he was harmless and let him go. After that, though, he did sneak out of Hungary and get to Mexico some way or other. Then he nearly starved down there waiting for a passport permit to get into the United States. Once he got here, he ate so much he got bloated. He's had a rough time of it, and he's so jumpy and jittery yet that he can't even give lectures. He hates to meet strangers, and if anyone starts staring at him, he tries to crawl inside his clothes. It's a shame, because I think he must have been a nice man before all this happened to him."

"He was anyway a damned good biochemist," Beulah Porter Cowys added.

"What do you teach?" Doan asked.

"Elementary physics. Very dull stuff."

A man came running up the front steps of the building and bounced through the front door. He sensed that there was someone in front of him, and he stopped so quickly he skidded, peering at them in a myopically eager way. He was all hands and feet and freckles, and his red hair was slicked down painfully flat except for three clumps at the back that stuck out like an untrimmed hedge. He spotted Melissa and gave another bounce and an embarrassed gulp.

"Oh! Hello, hello! Hello, Melissa! I was just going to drop into your office and—and say hello."

"You'd better say it here," Melissa advised. "My office has been liberated."

"Really?"

"Yes. The enemy is in possession."

"What enemy?"

"A party known as Handsome Lover Boy, alias Eric Trent."

"Trent," said the newcomer. "Oh, yes. He's the new meteorology man. I met him at the faculty lunch yesterday. He's very nice."

"He is not!"

"Isn't he?" the man asked anxiously.

"No! He's a boor and—and a cad!"

"Really?" said the man. "Was he rude to you, Melissa? Shall I go up and hit him in the face?"

"Never mind," Melissa said. "Mr. Doan, this is Frank Ames. He's an assistant professor of English. Mr. Doan is Handsome Lover Boy's bodyguard, Frank."

"How odd," Ames said absently. "Melissa, you haven't forgotten, have you? Tonight, I mean? Our date?"

"No, Frank. Just see that you don't forget"

"I certainly wouldn't forget anything that concerned you or— Oh! Your letter!" He commenced to fumble through his pockets. "It was in your slot over at Administration. . .I put it somewhere I wouldn't lose. . .Here!"

Melissa took the letter and opened it. "Well, well. A personal

missive from the president's office, if you please. And signed by
T. Ballard Bestwyck in person or a rubber stamp. . .Oh!
Ooooooh!"

"What?" asked Beulah Porter Cowys.

"Gluck-gluck-gluck," Melissa said in frustrated incoherence.
"Gluck! It says I have to exchange apartments in Pericles Pavilion with that—that—that—with Handsome Lover Boy because
the one I'm in is a double and his is a single and he needs more
room! Just after I've gotten mine decorated to suit me! I won't
do it! I—will—not—do—it!"

"Oh, yes, you will," said Beulah Porter Cowys.

"Why?" Melissa demanded defiantly.

"Because T. Ballard Bestwyck told you to, and T. Ballard
Bestwyck sits at God's right hand."

"Oh, damn!" said Melissa. "Oh, double damn-damn-damn!"

The moon was riding high, red and fat and swollen with its
own importance, when Frank Ames' dusty little coupe puttered
up the hill and pulled into the curb opposite the Pericles Pavilion.

Frank Ames turned off the coupe's motor. He swallowed and
took three long, deep breaths and then turned and stared at Melissa in a portentously concentrated manner. Melissa sighed and
wiggled a little on the slippery seat. She knew what was coming.
It always did.

"Melissa," said Frank Ames, "I have a very serious matter
which I wish to present to you for your consideration. I wish to
ask you—to entreat you—"

"Thank you for the dinner and the movie," Melissa said.

"No," said Frank Ames. "I mean, it was a pleasure, but that
isn't what I wanted to—"

"I had a very nice time," Melissa told him.

"What? Oh; that's nice, but Melissa, I feel that you and I are
ideally constituted to embark upon—"

Melissa opened the door on her side. "Don't bother to come
in with me, Frank. It's late, and I know you're as tired as I am.

The first day of the quarter is always a bore, isn't it?"

"What? Yes. Yes, indeed. But, Melissa, I haven't had a chance to tell you how I feel about—"

"Goodnight, Frank," said Melissa. "I've really got to run."

"But—but—but—"

"See you tomorrow!" said Melissa.

"Oh," said Frank Ames glumly, "Drat."

Melissa ran across the street. The Pericles Pavilion, in spite of its classically resounding title, was nothing but a small apartment house, a little ragged and run down at the heels. There was no point in keeping it up to snuff, because it had no competition, and besides no one but a few instructors and assistants lived there. It belonged to the university, and hence it came under the autocratic direction of T. Ballard Bestwyck, who subscribed to the theory that the payment of the most rent possible entitled the payer to the least comfort feasible because it was obvious to him that no one but an idiot would pay rent in the first place.

Melissa pushed through the squeaky double door and went on through the narrow L-shaped lobby and up the scuffed stairs to the second floor. She hadn't moved out of her apartment as yet. She knew very well that there was no question of whether she would move—just a matter of when. But nonetheless she was determined to fight as stubborn a delaying action as possible.

She was directly in front of the apartment, fumbling for the key in her purse, when she noticed that the door was not quite closed. Melissa drew in her breath slowly. She thought of a great many lurid words and applied them all to a personality known as Handsome Lover Boy.

Very quietly she pushed the door open wider. The light in her living room was not on, and the furniture looked distorted and unfamiliar. The door of her bedroom was open, and there was a light in there—dim and bluish and indistinct. Melissa knew that this light came from the reading lamp clamped on the head of her bed, and she began to seethe inside at the mere thought.

She tiptoed across the living room and stopped in the bedroom doorway. The light did come from her reading lamp, and it reflected from the brightly patterned spread on her bed and from the brightly painted face of the little Spanish clock on her night table. Melissa saw, without noticing, that the gilt hands of the clock were lined up at midnight exactly.

There was a man standing in front of her dresser with his back to her. Melissa opened her mouth, but she didn't speak. There was something queer about this man.

Melissa swallowed against the sudden tightness in her throat. The man's head was black—all black—and it was distorted in back into an ugly knotted lump. His hands were black, too—a different kind of black, smooth and shiny and ridged. He was staring down at a pair of Melissa's nylon stockings that dribbled limply between his black, clumsy fingers.

The Spanish clock whirred very softly to itself and then tinkled out its dusty-sweet little Andalusian peasant tune. The black man made a startled sound deep in his throat. He whirled half-around, and one of his shiny hands reached out for the clock.

"No!" Melissa cried involuntarily.

The black man kept right on turning until he faced her. Melissa knew now what made the blackness of his head. He was wearing a stocking mask, pulled tight and knotted at the back of his neck. There were eyeholes in it, and he was watching her through them. He was wearing black leather gloves on his hands.

He made no sound at all. Melissa backed up a step, and then he moved, coming at her with a deadly, animal-like swiftness.

Melissa screamed—once.

CHAPTER TWO

IT WAS TWENTY-THREE MINUTES AFTER eleven when Eric Trent closed the textbook he was reading with a sharp, disgusted snap and said, "I've been reading the same page for the last half hour, and it still doesn't make sense. Let's go get a beer."

Doan had been lying on his back on the chesterfield with his hands folded across his chest. He sat up instantly and started hunting around for his shoes.

"Now you're talking," he said enthusiastically.

Carstairs was sprawled all over the floor in front of the door. He sat up, too.

"Trent and I are going to the library and get some books," Doan told him.

Carstairs watched him.

"Don't look so damned skeptical!" Doan shouted. "I can read. And dogs aren't allowed in the library, so just relax and lie down again. You're staying here."

Carstairs stood up and turned his back and put his nose against the door.

"All right, all right," Doan said. "Hurry up, Trent. The bars close up in this cockeyed state at midnight."

He opened the door, and Carstairs preceded them down the long hall. This apartment was on the third floor, and there was no elevator. There were no elevators in any of the university buildings with the exception of those frequented by T. Ballard Bestwyck. He did not believe in pampering the lower classes. Doan and Trent, with Carstairs still ahead of them, went down the stairs past Melissa's floor, and on down the first flight and out through the lobby.

Trent's car—a small and shabby two-door sedan—was parked at the curb fifty yards north of Pericles Pavilion. Doan opened the door on the right side and hitched the seat forward.

"Get in back," he ordered. "Snap it up."

Carstairs climbed in distrustfully.

Doan popped the seat back into place and slid into it. "Hurry up. It's half-past eleven."

Trent started the car, and they drove through the narrow, sharply curved residential streets that bordered the university and then out on the smooth, wide sweep of the boulevard that ran south of the campus.

"There's a place," said Doan. "Kerrigan's Klub Kar. Under the green neon sign ahead."

"All right," said Trent absently. He drove the car into the empty graveled lot beside the building and parked.

"Roll your window up about three-quarters of the way and get out and shut your door," Doan said casually. He was lounging back in the seat with his hands folded back of his neck.

Trent looked at him curiously. "Okay."

Doan waited until Trent's door was shut, and then he slipped the catch on the door next to him with his knee. In one smooth motion, he darted out of the car and slammed the door shut behind him. He was not a split second too soon. Carstairs broad, moist muzzle slapped against the inside of the glass an instant after the door thumped shut. His eyes glared through at them, greenishly malignant.

"What's the idea?" Trent asked.

"He's a dry," Doan explained. "He hates liquor. I don't like to take him in bars because he raises hell. He sneers at the customers and barks at the bartender and tips over tables. Hurry up. It's twenty minutes to twelve."

They went up three steps and into a long, dreary room with a bar running along the length of one wall. The place was empty except for the bartender and one chummy customer. The chummy customer hailed them with a loud and lonesome cheer.

"Hiya! Hi there, fellas! Have a drink, huh?"

"Now, Bert," said the bartender.

"Well, I know that guy there," said Bert. "I sure do know that guy. I sure seen his face before lots of times. Sure. Now wait a minute. Don't rush me." He came weaving along the bar. "Hi, fella! I seen you before, ain't I, huh? Huh?"

"Lay off, Bert," said the bartender.

"Yee-hoo!" Bert yelled joyously. "I got it! I know where I saw you! In all them ads for all that face cream junk! Sure! How are you, little old Handsome little old Lover little old Boy? Woo-woo-woo!"

Eric Trent hit him on the side of the neck with the edge of his palm. Bert came apart at the seams. He hit the floor so hard he bounced. After that he didn't move at all.

"Here!" the bartender said indignantly. "What's the idea? He's my best customer. I recognize your face myself. If you want to marry some old crow for her dough and advertise it in all the magazines, you've got no right to get sore if people rib you about it. What did you do to Bert?"

"This," said Trent.

The bartender's jaw smacked against the edge of the bar, and then he slid gently and slowly down out of sight behind it.

"Let's get out of here," Trent said.

"I think maybe that's a good idea," Doan agreed reluctantly, looking at the electric clock behind the bar.

It was thirteen minutes of twelve.

They went back outside, and Doan opened the left door of the sedan.

"Oh, stop snorting at me," he ordered. "I didn't have anything to drink—not even a beer. Get in the back."

Carstairs climbed over the seat, muttering to himself.

Doan got in. "We'll have to hurry," he said. "It's almost midnight."

Trent pushed the starter. "I've lost my thirst."

"Well, I haven't," said Doan. "Drive around fast and find a place where I can pick up a pint."

Trent drove out on the boulevard. "I've got a bottle at home you can have."

"Where?" Doan demanded. "I searched that apartment from stem to stern the other morning when I was suddenly taken with a hangover."

"That big green book in my bookcase—the one with the Greek lettering on it—is a fake. It's hollow. There's a fifth of bourbon in it."

"Do tell," said Doan. "Have you got any more literature like that?"

"No. I wouldn't have that except for the fact that my wife bought it for me."

"She's very thoughtful of you," Doan told him. "She not only gives you liquor, but she also provides you with a party named Doan to drink it."

"Yes," said Trent.

They drove back through the winding residential streets. Trent parked the car at the curb near the Pericles Pavilion, where it had been before. Garages are an affectation in Southern California and aren't used except by people who wish to impress, or don't trust, their neighbors.

"Come on, stupid," Doan said, holding the door open for Carstairs.

The three of them were on the steps of the apartment building when the chimes in the university chapel tower began to boom lugubriously.

"Twelve o'clock," said Doan, pushing through the doors into the lobby, "and all's well."

And then the three of them stopped short.

"What was that?" Trent demanded.

"A dame screaming," said Doan. "There must be a wifebeater hidden around this rat trap somewhere."

He was watching Carstairs. Carstairs had his head raised alertly. His ears were pricked forward, and a muscle quivered nervously in his shoulder.

"Find them," said Doan.

Carstairs and Doan both moved so fast then that Trent was caught flatfooted. Carstairs was at the top of the first flight of stairs and Doan was halfway up before Trent could get started. He pounded after them, taking the steps three at a jump. He turned out into the hall at the top.

Doan was halfway along it, standing in front of an open apartment door. He had his right hand inside the front of his coat. Trent pulled up behind him and stared over his shoulder.

Melissa was lying in a bedraggled heap in the middle of the living room floor. Her eyes were shut and her mouth was open and her legs were sprawled immodestly. Carstairs was just inside the door, watching her with his head lowered and one huge paw raised.

"What?" said Trent. "What was . . . Why, it's that homely girl who wanted me to give her my office! What's the matter with her? What happened to her?"

"Somebody popped her on the jaw," Doan said absently, "and knocked her cold. See where her heel dragged in front of the bedroom door?"

Trent looked at the heel mark and then he looked down at Melissa. "Well, not so homely." He twisted his head around and took a step across the room. "In fact, considered from the proper angle, rather nice. I've seen the time when I could use something like this. I'd prefer her conscious, of course."

"Huh," said Doan. "From what I hear, when she's conscious she doesn't prefer you."

Carstairs swung about to stare up at Doan and give him an inquiring look.

Doan nodded. "Yeah. Let's find the bird who did the bopping."

Carstairs walked out into the hall, still eyeing Doan.

"Go on," said Doan. "Get him."

Carstairs started with a lunge and headed down the hall toward the back of the building like an arrow out of a bow.

"Pick up the doll and paste her together," Doan said to Trent. "We're busy."

Doan turned and ran back down the front stairs. He skidded to a stop in the lobby, listening. He was holding a .38 Colt Police Positive in his right hand now.

Carstairs bayed from the back of the building.

"Yeah!" said Doan.

He ran back through the lower hall, whirled around a corner with the revolver up and poised. Carstairs was standing up against a closed door further along, pawing at its panels with the claws of both front paws.

"Get away," said Doan, shouldering him aside. "This is the cellar, I think. Watch it."

He pulled the door open, staying partially behind it. There was nothing on the other side but pitch darkness. Carstairs dove heedlessly right into it. There was a rumble and a bump as he hit a lower level and then the skitter of his claws on cement.

"Wait until I find the light, you fool," Doan ordered.

Carstairs began to bellow in furious frustration.

"All right," said Doan.

He pushed ahead into the blackness, located steps under his feet, and went stumbling and sliding down them, waving both arms wildly over his head. He hit bottom and fell headlong over something that rattled and rolled tinnily.

Carstairs was raising racketing echoes somewhere in front of him.

Doan scrambled to his feet and groped blindly forward until he bumped into Carstairs and then into another closed door. He found the catch and pulled the door back. Fresh, cool air puffed into his face, and Carstairs lurched up a half flight of cement steps and out into the open. Doan ran up after him and came out in the back areaway of the apartment house. It was surrounded by a high, thick hedge.

An opening showed dimly at Doan's right, and he headed for it. A clothesline brushed his hair neatly and eerily, and then he burst through the opening and stumbled on the rough surface of a narrow alley. Carstairs made a motionless, stilt-legged shadow ten feet away. He snorted at Doan in a disgusted way.

"Lost him, huh?" said Doan. "Well, don't just stand there with your teeth in your mouth. Get out and beat around in the weeds in that lot. Go on. Hike."

Carstairs faded silently into the darkness.

Doan began to walk very cautiously down the alley, slipping silently along with his head half-turned so he could watch in both directions, searching each shadow. He had gone about twenty yards when something whispered spitefully past his ear and something else twitched the cuff of his coatsleeve and a third something drew a line across the telephone pole he was touching with his left hand.

Doan was falling by that time, and as he dropped he heard the reports—three of them very close together, but sharp and nastily distinct. He flattened himself on the dirt, hiding his face in the crook of his elbow. He was swearing at himself in a mumbling undertone.

Carstairs came down the alley, running low and very fast and making fierce little grunting sounds. Doan thrust out his arm and caught Carstairs halfway up his front legs. Carstairs did a complete somersault in the air and came down flat on his back with a breathless "Ga-whoomp."

Doan hitched forward and fell across him. "Be still!" he snarled. "Quiet!"

They lay there in a rigid, motionless tangle. In a couple of moments, a car starter ground somewhere close. The engine caught with a choked roar, and then tires made a long wailing protest as the car whirled around a corner. The sound died away.

"Wow," said Doan softly, sitting up.

Carstairs sat up, too, and glared at him.

"Oh, relax," said Doan. "Why do you act so stupid? That boy had a gun, and he certainly knows how to use it. He was just on the other side of that street light ahead. If you had run out under that light, he'd have picked you off like a duck on a rock."

Carstairs grunted.

"The same to you," said Doan. "I certainly get a lot of thanks for all the care and attention I lavish—what's the matter with you now?"

Carstairs rumbled deep in his throat. His head was turned away from Doan, and he was watching an apartment-size trash can on the other side of the alley. The lid of the can was tipped drunkenly to one side.

Doan was on his feet instantly. The hammer of his revolver made a soft, metallic click.

"Come out of that," he said.

There was no answer—no sound.

Doan approached the can, circling. Close to it, he put his right foot against the upper part and heaved. The lid fell off with a rattling clangor. The can tilted past its balance line and fell suddenly on its side.

Doan's breath hissed through his teeth. A foot protruded from the open end of the can—a man's foot clad in a tan sport shoe. The foot was queerly limp.

It didn't move.

Leaning down suddenly, Doan took hold of the foot and jerked hard. The rest of the man's body slid loosely and easily out of the can.

"This is nice, too," said Doan. "Oh, this is just dandy."

He found a match and snapped it on his thumbnail. The man's throat had been cut with one deft, neat slash that began under his ear and slanted down and across. His face was smeared thickly with blood, but Doan recognized him at once. He was Frank Ames. He was dead.

Doan dropped the match and nodded solemnly at Carstairs. "The bird we were chasing so merrily carries a knife and a gun, and he operates in a very fancy way with both or either. I don't think we would care to know him any better, but I'm afraid we're going to."

Carstairs began to scratch himself.

Doan and Carstairs came into the apartment building through the front door. The lobby was as empty and shabby as it had been before and would be again, and they were heading for the stairs when the first door on the lower hall opened and two faces peered out at them.

That is, Doan saw two faces. Or, rather, he saw one face multiplied by two—one above the other. It was very uncanny. The two faces duplicated each other exactly. They were round, pink-cheeked, feminine, middle-aged faces. They had braided gray hair tied with blue ribbons. They had blue, frightened eyes that peered at Doan through identical pairs of pince-nez spectacles.

The short hairs at the back of Doan's neck rose and prickled alarmingly. Carstairs made a startled noise through his nose and ducked behind Doan's legs.

"Hello," said the faces.

Doan swallowed. "Hello," he said faintly.

"We are the Misses Aldrich," said the faces.

"Are—are there two of you?" Doan asked.

"Yes. We're twins."

"Oh," said Doan, breathing again. He looked back and down at Carstairs. "You big coward."

"We are specialists," said the Aldriches in fascinating unison, "in the emotional and social conditioning of pre-school-age children. We teach that at the university. To students of education."

"I see," said Doan.

"We heard noises. We heard screams and loud, raucous shouting. We were frightened."

"I'm sorry," said Doan.

"We think we even heard some shots. Do you think you heard some shots, too?"

"Yes," said Doan. "I think I did."

"Do you think there might be some intoxicated persons at large on the premises?"

"I couldn't say," Doan told them.

"Do you think we are in danger?"

"I hardly think so," said Doan.

"Thank you," said the Aldriches, "for reassuring us. You are very kind."

"Thank you," said Doan.

"You have a very large dog."

"Yes," Doan admitted. "Unfortunately."

"We do not have a dog."

"You're lucky."

"But we like dogs very much. Will you be so kind as to allow us to pet your dog at some more appropriate time?"

"I will," said Doan, "but of course the important question is whether or not he will. He doesn't like to be petted. He thinks it demeans him. And now, if you'll excuse me, I'll go up and look into the screaming at a little closer range."

"Be very careful."

"Indeed, I will."

"Good night."

"Good night," said Doan.

He nudged Carstairs with his knee, and the two of them went up the stairs and along the hall to Melissa's apartment. The door was ajar, and Doan pushed it open wider and looked in.

Melissa was lying on the chesterfield, propped up with some wadded pillows. Her hair straggled dankly down over her cheeks, and her mascara had run in futuristic streaks. She looked very repulsive. She was holding an ice bag against the left side of her face, and in the other hand she held a tall glass of murkily powerful looking liquid. She sipped the liquid with little blubbering sounds and glared at Doan. Her eyes weren't focusing very efficiently.

Beulah Porter Cowys was hovering over Melissa, twitching at the pillows and making little croaking sounds that were meant to be soothing. Eric Trent was standing against the opposite wall, trying to appear at ease and find a place to put his hands.

"Well!" said Beulah Porter Cowys. "The great, late detective! What have you been doing all this time—hiding in a dark closet?"

"No," said Doan, "but there was a moment there when I wished I had one to hide in." He nodded at Melissa. "How do you feel now?"

"How do you suppose?"

Beulah Porter Cowys said, "That decorative dimwit dumped a barrel of water in her face."

"It was a glass of water," Trent corrected coldly.

"It was too much, anyway."

"I thought that was the proper remedy in the case of mild shock."

"Well, stop thinking," Beulah Porter Cowys advised. "You aren't equipped for it."

"Mild shock!" Melissa echoed thickly. "What are you talking about? I didn't faint. I was knocked out."

"I'm sorry," said Trent. "I was trying to help you the best way I knew."

"Oh, yeah? What are you doing here, anyway? Lurking and throwing water at people? I suppose you think you can put me out of my apartment while I'm too weak to resist."

"What?" said Trent blankly.

"Oh, stop trying to act innocent. I'm nauseated enough already."

"I don't know what you're talking about," Trent told her.

"It's not important now, anyway, is it?" Doan said quickly. "I mean, there's the matter of this prowler to consider."

Trent looked at him. "I heard some shots. Were you shooting at him?"

"No," said Doan. "On the contrary."

"Oh, phooey with an olive," said Beulah Porter Cowys. "It was probably just a car backfiring."

"Then this car backfired bullets," Doan told her, "and that's not all it did, either. I'm afraid we're going to have to call the police."

"I already have," said Trent. "The first thing."

"Uh!" Doan grunted. "Which police did you call?"

"The sheriff's office—the university substation."

"Oh—oh," said Doan. "Oh—oh—oh."

"What's the matter?" Trent demanded.

"A guy named Humphrey is the deputy-in-charge there. And he doesn't like me any at all."

"Why not?" Beulah Porter Cowys demanded. "Aside from the fact that liking you is a pretty difficult thing to do."

"You're kind to say so," Doan said. "Humphrey has a grudge against me because he hates Carstairs. Carstairs spends nine-tenths of his time alienating people and making enemies. He humiliated Humphrey, and that's a thing that no cop can take. At least, no cop named Humphrey."

"How did he do it?"

"Well," said Doan, "it's like this. Since my youth I have been subject to periodic attacks of vertigo, during which I find it difficult to walk straight. Many callous and uninformed characters— like Carstairs, for instance—think these attacks are due to drinking alcohol in large quantities, but of course that's nonsense."

"Oh, certainly," said Beulah Porter Cowys.

"At the time I'm talking about, by the merest and sheerest coincidence, I was seized by one of my attacks while I was sitting at a bar. So I started home, and I was sort of tacking and veering down the street when Humphrey spotted me. Carstairs, the cad, won't even walk with me when I'm in the throes of one of my attacks for fear people will connect the two of us. He pretends he doesn't know me. This time he was tagging along about fifty yards behind me."

"This is getting good," said Beulah Porter Cowys. "Go on."

"Humphrey grabbed me. He was in plainclothes, and he was connected with homicide then, and it was none of his affair whether I was drunk—I mean, sick—or not. That's what I told him, and so he started to shove me around, and Carstairs came up and bit him in the pants."

"In the pants?" Beulah Porter Cowys repeated.

"Yes. He didn't touch Humphrey. He just tore the seat clear out of his pants. It was broad daylight on a busy street, and Humphrey collected quite an audience. That made him mad. He's still mad."

"Oh, well," said Beulah Porter Cowys, "maybe he won't be on duty tonight"

"He's always on duty. He never sleeps, for fear he might miss out on a chance to arrest someone. He loves to arrest people. He'll arrest me as soon as he sees me."

"That's nonsense," said Trent. "Policemen don't go around arresting people just because they have a grudge against them."

"Ha?" said Doan. "May I use your telephone, Melissa?"

Humphrey was as round and smooth and soft as a custard pie. He came huffing importantly into the apartment, flapping his hat indignantly in his hand, with three uniformed deputies trailing right behind him.

"Now!" he barked. "What's all this nonsense about a prowler—"

He saw Carstairs. There was a pregnant, crackling silence, and then Humphrey's neck began to puff pinkly above his shirt collar.

Carstairs was sitting down, leaning against the wall with his eyes shut, dozing. After awhile he opened one eye and regarded Humphrey in a critical, coldly detached way, and then shut the eye again and went on dozing.

Humphrey turned his head slowly and carefully, with the air of a man who knows there is a coiled rattlesnake near him somewhere. Doan was sitting sprawled out in the lounge chair in tie corner.

"There he is," said Humphrey. "That's the guy. Put the cuffs on him."

One of the deputies stepped forward alertly, pulling his handcuffs from their leather case on the back of his belt. Doan held out his hands amiably, and the cuffs snapped around his wrists.

"Search him," Humphrey ordered.

"It's in my waistband," Doan volunteered.

The deputy found the revolver. "It's a .38 Police Positive," he reported.

"And I've got a license to carry it," said Doan.

"You won't have long," Humphrey told him. "All right, you people. You'll have to appear at his arraignment. That'll be in the court in downtown Los Angeles, probably on Wednesday morning. The district attorney's office will get in touch with you. Bring him along, boys."

"Here!" Eric Trent shouted. "What do you think you're doing?"

Humphrey looked at him. "Who're you?"

"My name is Eric Trent. Doan warned me you'd act like this, but I was stupid enough to think you'd have better sense. Doan ate dinner with me, and he was with me continuously from that time up to the time we heard this woman—What's your name, you?"

"It's Melissa Gregory, in case it's any of your business, you."

"Up to the time we heard this Melissa Gregory scream," Trent went on, paying no attention to her tone.

"Trying to alibi him, eh?" said Humphrey. "That just makes you an accessory, bub. And you've got a record, too, haven't you? I've seen your picture before."

"Sir," said one of the deputies.

Humphrey looked at him. "What do you want?"

"He's Handsome Lover Boy."

"What?"

"He's the guy in those cold cream ads."

"Well, I'll be damned," said Humphrey. "So you pose for ads when you're not prowling, eh?"

"Sir," said the deputy.

"Now what?"

"He's really married to that woman—that Heloise of Hollywood. It was in the papers—in the society news—a couple of years back. My wife read it to me."

"Hmmm," said Humphrey, staring at Trent. "Is that a fact? Are you really her husband?"

"Yes," said Trent tightly.

"Hmmm," said Humphrey. "Hmmm." He spun around suddenly and pointed at Doan. "Who hired you?"

"You'll find out," said Doan, "in due course."

"I'll find out right now!"

"My wife hired him," Trent said.

"To do what?"

"To watch me."

"Ah," said Humphrey. "And of course he's playing both ends against the middle as usual. He always does. When anyone hires him to watch someone else, he always runs around to the second party and tells them and then collects from each of them for watching the other. Don't you?"

"Sure," said Doan.

Melissa sat up on the couch. "Listen, you," she said loudly and clearly. "You were called here to investigate a masked prowler who attacked me. Are you going to do that, or are you going to get the hell out of my apartment?"

"Melissa!" Beulah Porter Cowys gasped.

"I mean it," said Melissa. "I'm serious. I've had my nose rubbed in this teak-headed Trent's nasty personal affairs until I'm good and sick of him and them."

"Doan is the prowler," Humphrey told her.

"He is not!"

"Well, then Trent is."

"He isn't, either!"

"How do you know—if the guy was masked?"

"Because he wasn't as tall as Trent nor as fat as Doan."

"You're just trying to make things difficult for me," Humphrey complained.

"I'll make them more difficult," said Doan. "There's a murdered man in an ashcan out in the alley in back."

"Ah-ha!" Humphrey gloated, rubbing his hands. "You heard that confession, all of you? You're witnesses. I've always hoped for a chance to peek at you in the gas chamber, Doan. Who'd you kill? You might as well tell the truth, because I won't believe what you say, anyway."

"I didn't kill anyone," said Doan. "The prowler did it on his way out."

Humphrey waved his hand. "A detail. I know you're the prowler. Who is the guy, and why did you knock him off?"

"His name is Frank Ames."

"Oh!" Melissa gasped.

"Frank," said Beulah Porter Cowys, swallowing with a little croaking sound. "Gee."

"Frank Ames," Trent repeated thoughtfully. "I met someone by that name at the faculty lunch . . . Isn't he a redhaired chap? English assistant?"

"That's the one," said Doan.

"Why did you murder him?" Humphrey demanded.

"I just got through telling you I didn't. The prowler did."

"Sure, sure," said Humphrey. "Don't quibble. Just tell me why it happened."

"I'm not sure why. Ames doesn't live here, but I think he

must have been visiting someone in the building."

"M-me," said Melissa. "He took me to dinner and the m-movies."

"That's it," said Doan. "Which way did he bring you home——did he drive up the hill?"

"Yes."

Doan nodded at Humphrey. "Here's what happened, then. He swung his car around in a U-turn in the middle of the street. His headlights swung across that alley just as the prowler was coming out of the back areaway. Ames saw him. I think probably the prowler either had taken off or was taking off his mask. He wouldn't want to run around the streets with it on."

"You mean, Ames recognized you?" Humphrey asked.

"I think he must have recognized the prowler. Otherwise Ames wouldn't have gotten out of his car, and he did. His car is headed into the curb ten feet this way from the alley with the door still open. He jumped out and went to find out what the prowler was up to. If he hadn't known the prowler and recognized him, the prowler would just have batted him one like he did Melissa, instead of cutting his throat."

Humphrey nodded at two of the deputies. "Go take a look. See how much of this he's making up."

The two deputies ducked out the door.

Melissa was bent double. "It was my—my—my fault. . ."

Humphrey pounced. "What? What's that? Speak up."

"Shut up," said Beulah Porter Cowys. "Don't pay any attention to this fat boob, Melissa. Don't say anything at all if you don't want to."

Melissa said slowly, getting the words out with enormous effort: "He tried to ask me to marry him. He had many times—before. I liked him, but . . .this time I avoided—I slipped away. Oh, Beulah!"

Beulah Porter Cowys seized her competently by the shoulders. "Right in here, honey. Come on." She boosted Melissa to her feet and headed her for the bedroom.

"Wait, now!" Humphrey shouted. "About this prowler.

What kind of a mask did he have on?"

"A stocking—a silk stocking. Black. Over his whole head."

"Whole head," said Humphrey. "Whole head. . .What about the hands? Did you see them?"

"Gloves. Black shiny gloves."

"That's all," said Beulah Porter Cowys, shepherding Melissa into the bedroom and slamming the door.

"Who is that dame?" Humphrey asked. "The old scrawny one?"

"Beulah Porter Cowys," Trent told him.

"Where'd she come from?"

"She lives down the hall. She heard Melissa Gregory scream and came to see what was wrong."

"She did, did she?" said Humphrey. "Does she ever wear slacks?"

"No," said Doan.

"Yes," said Trent at the same time. He looked at Doan, startled. "What?"

Doan said wearily: "Humphrey is going off into another of his dreams. The prowler wasn't Beulah Porter Cowys because I was chasing the prowler."

"Oh, yeah?" said Humphrey. "It could have been her—with gloves to hide her nail polish and a stocking over her noggin to hide her long hair."

"Smoke another pipe," Doan advised.

"Okay, smarty," said Humphrey. "Did you see this prowler? I mean, did you pass a mirror on your way out?"

"No," said Doan, "but I can give you a handy item of information about him. He packs a gun as well as a knife. It's a .22, and it's an automatic, so it's probably a Colt Woodsman. He's very handy with it. If you'll look, you'll find three ejected shells on the other side of the street light north of the building."

"Now you're dreaming. Why would he want to pack a pea-shooter like a .22?"

"If you can shoot like he can, you don't need anything bigger."

Beulah Porter Cowys came out of the bedroom. "You'll have

to adjourn this bull session. Melissa is all shot to pieces. Scat."

"Not so fast," said Humphrey. "Just how well do you know Doan, eh?"

"Just as well as I want to," said Beulah Porter Cowys, "and that's hardly at all."

One of the uniformed deputies squeezed through the front door. "The body is there, sir, and so is the car. It's registered in Ames' name. But look what I found back of the seat."

In front of him, balanced like a tray, he was carrying a very large, thick book with a flossy hand-carved leather cover. The deputy was supporting it with the tips of his fingers. On the cover, stamped in gold, was the legend: THE PATHWAY TO PERFECTION—HELOISE OF HOLLYWOOD.

"I peeked in it," said the deputy. "It tells how to get rid of your wrinkles if you're an old dame and got lots."

"Hmmm," said Humphrey. "Did your wife know Ames, Trent?"

"I don't think so," said Trent.

"She did," said Doan. "He was working for her."

"What?" said Beulah Porter Cowys incredulously. "Frank working for Heloise of Hollywood? You're just completely nuts!"

"Not this time," Doan told her. "She's getting together a new advertising campaign. It's going to be all about middle-aged women who had a big influence on history—had poems written to them and lakes named after them and wars started on account of them and all like that. Ames was doing the research for her."

"How do you know?" Beulah Porter Cowys demanded.

"Because Heloise told me so."

"Hmmm," said Humphrey. "Hmmmm. This case is beginning to develop some angles. Now suppose Ames was getting chummy with Trent's wife, and Trent found it out from Doan and hired Doan to hide in that alley and then lured Ames. . ."

"Here we go again," said Doan.

Humphrey ignored him. "Or suppose Doan told Heloise that her husband was getting chummy with this Melissa Gregory, and Heloise dropped in here to look around. Of course, Doan would cover for Heloise, because he could shake her down for plenty, and this Melissa would try to throw me off because she doesn't want any scandal. And Ames recognized Heloise and tried a little shaking down of his own, and Doan got mad about that. . ."

"Is this man crazy or something?" Trent demanded.

"He's certainly something," Doan agreed.

The telephone rang in the bedroom, and Humphrey and Beulah Porter Cowys made a simultaneous dash for it. Melissa was lying face down on the bed, her face buried in her arms. Beulah Porter Cowys leaned over her and grabbed the phone.

"Here!" Humphrey shouted. "Give me that! I warn you now—"

"Shut up," said Beulah Porter Cowys, kicking at him. "Get away. . .Hello . . .Yes . . .Is he a fat, pig-faced character with a big mouth? . . . Yes, he's here." She extended the telephone toward Humphrey. "It's for you."

"Hello!" Humphrey bellowed. "Who are—Who? . . . Yes, sir . . . Yes, sir . . . Yes, sir . . . T. Ballard Bestwyck and the mayor and the president of the Chamber of Commerce and the district attorney—all of them? But Doan doesn't know them . . . Yes, sir. I know they know you . . . Yes, sir . . . Yes, sir . . . But there's been a murder, and Doan is involved—Yes, sir . . . Yes, sir . . . At once, sir."

Humphrey handed the phone back to Beulah Porter Cowys. He looked a little wilted. He went back into the living room and stared at Doan with his shoulders hunched and his lower lip stuck out.

"Hello there, Humphrey," said Doan.

Humphrey grunted. "Take the cuffs off him," he said drearily.

The deputy who wasn't carrying the book unlocked the handcuffs.

"Give me my gun," Doan requested.

Humphrey nodded reluctantly, and the deputy handed over the Police Positive. Doan put it in his waistband.

"I don't know yet how you got all that big noise to front for you," Humphrey told him bitterly, "but, oh, you just wait. There'll come a day. And in the meantime—"

Humphrey spun around suddenly and kicked viciously at the spot where Carstairs had been sitting an instant before. Carstairs wasn't there now. Humphrey's foot went through the space he had been occupying and hit the wall hard.

"Oooh-woooo!" Humphrey bellowed.

Carstairs looked out from behind Doan's chair and regarded him with an air of polite inquiry.

Melissa appeared in the bedroom doorway, holding on to both sides of it for support. "You get out of my apartment—all of you!"

Humphrey was standing on one foot, holding the other with both hands. "Now wait a minute. I've got to look for clues—"

"Get out of here!"

Eric Trent said, "I don't think you should stay alone—"

"Shut up, you! Get out!"

Beulah Porter Cowys said, "I'll stay with—"

"Beulah, no! I don't want *anyone* here! I Just want everyone to leave me *alone!* Now, go away! Go home! All of you! Get out!"

"Let me leave Carstairs here," Doan said. "He won't bother you, and he won't let anyone in you don't want in."

"All right, all right, all right!"

Doan pointed his finger at Carstairs. "You stay. Do you hear? No one comes in unless she says so."

Carstairs was leaning against the wall again, dozing. He didn't open his eyes.

Trent said: "I still don't think—"

"Get out, get out, get out!" Melissa screamed.

She ran at them and pushed and shoved indiscriminately. They all bumbled and stumbled out into the hall, and she slammed the door and locked it and then propped a chair under the knob.

She sighed shakily, then. Her knees didn't feel like they belonged to her. She went into the bedroom, dragging her heels, and began to undress.

She was unhooking her brassiere when there was a sudden

loud and juicy plop from the direction of the kitchen. Melissa stiffened rigidly, feeling her heart inflate like a balloon, and then she whirled around and ran through the living room to the kitchen doorway. She snapped on the light.

The refrigerator door was wide open, and on the floor in front of it there was a large glass bowl of potato salad, wrong side up. Carstairs was regarding this last phenomenon with an air of incredulous amazement.

"You—you!" Melissa shouted. "You thief! You food robber!"

She slashed at him with the brassiere. He dodged that with negligent ease. Melissa's knees gave out entirely, and she sat down and began to bawl, pounding the floor with her fists. Carstairs stared at her, aghast at this unseemly display of emotion, and then stalked into the living room, picking up his feet queasily.

After awhile, Melissa's sobs tapered off in to whimpering sniffles. She got up wearily and picked up the potato salad and wiped the floor.

Shutting the refrigerator door, she went back into the living room. Carstairs was nowhere in sight. Melissa went into the bedroom.

"You!" she shrieked. "Get off that bed! You're not going to sleep—Get off ! Get out!"

Carstairs retreated into the living room.

"On the floor!" Melissa shouted. "That's where you're going to sleep! Lie *down!*"

Carstairs bent his legs slightly and then let himself go and hit the floor hard enough to rattle the windowpanes. He rolled over on his side and commenced to snore instantly.

"Oh," said Melissa. "Oh, dear."

Melissa slept without the hindrance of pajamas or nightgowns or other such impedimenta, and consequently she was in the best condition possible to get the full benefit of Carstairs' nose when he placed it precisely between her shoulder blades. She came out of the dim, pleasant shadows of her private dream world in one hair-raising leap.

"What—what—what—"she gabbled, sitting up and kicking frantically at the covers.

Carstairs backed away from the bed. The sun was pushing bright, inquisitive fingers through the half-closed slats of the venetian blinds.

"You!" said Melissa. "I'll break every bone—Oooooh!" She felt the side of her face in a gently experimental way. Her jaw was hot and puffed and sore. It felt awful. Her mouth didn't taste at all good, either.

"Oh—oh—oh," said Melissa miserably. She dug at her eyes with her fists and then squinted painfully at the little Spanish clock. "Ten minutes of seven! What do you mean by waking me up at the crack of dawn, you stupid brainless monstrosity?"

Carstairs continued to regard her with an air of urgency.

"What's wrong with you?" Melissa demanded.

Carstairs lifted one forefoot and then the other in a painfully anxious way.

"Oh!" said Melissa. "You want to go, don't you! And the door downstairs is closed . . . Oh, damn! All right, all right. Wait until I get dressed."

She went into the bathroom and looked in the mirror and nearly frightened herself to death. Her cheek was inflated ludicrously, and along the lower side it was beginning to exhibit an interesting tinge of purple.

Carstairs whiffled from near the front door.

"All right," said Melissa, hurrying.

She put on some slacks and moccasins and a sweater and swiped at her hair with a comb and then went out into the living room. Carstairs was standing with his knees bent and his nose pressed against the front door.

Melissa opened it for him, and Carstairs shot down the hall and raised rumbling echoes on the stairs. He was waiting unwillingly at the front door of the building when Melissa got there. She opened the door for him. Carstairs slipped through and dove gratefully into the shrubbery that circled the building.

Melissa sat down on the steps. She found a cigarette and a

match in the pocket of her slacks. The cigarette tasted like under-
done steel filings.

It was one of those spring mornings in Southern California
that are so incredibly beautiful they seem indecent in some vague
way. The sun was just clearing the last of the night mist out of
the sky, and the palm trees—like king-sized, upended feather
dusters—nodded and dipped in polite unison at the urge of a softly
caressing breeze.

Carstairs peered out the shrubbery to make sure Melissa was
still waiting for him and then disappeared again. The door clicked
in back of Melissa, and the Aldrich twins appeared. They looked
at Melissa, taking in the slacks and the cigarette and the strag-
gling hair and the swollen cheek. They smiled in a patient, for-
giving way.

"Good morning," they said.

"Morning," said Melissa.

"It's a nice day."

"Is it?" Melissa asked.

Carstairs came out of the shrubbery and sat down on the steps
beside Melissa with a luxurious, replete sigh.

The Aldriches said, "That is the large dog which belongs to
the plump, pleasant-spoken man who rooms with Mr. Eric Trent."

"Yes," Melissa admitted. "His name is Doan. The man's. The
dog's name is Carstairs."

"Mr. Eric Trent is very handsome," said the Aldriches.

"So they say."

"We understand that he is married."

"I understand that, too."

"Hmmm," said the Aldriches. They watched her for a moment, and then they looked at Carstairs. "Mr. Doan intimated
that we might pet him."

"Go right ahead," Melissa invited.

"Here, Carstairs," said the Aldriches. "Here, nice dog."

Carstairs watched them for a moment, obviously weighing
alternatives. Finally he got up and stepped over to them. He per-
mitted them three pats each, and then he went back and sat down

with the air of a person who has done his duty.

"We must go now," said the Aldriches. "We always walk before breakfast. Early to bed and early to rise, you know."

"I know," Melissa agreed.

They went down the steps and along the walk. They were exactly the same height, and they walked in step.

The door clicked again, and Beulah Porter Cowys came out.

"Are they gone for good?" she asked. "They're a little too plural for me at this hour."

"What are you doing out so early?"

"I've got to set up the lab for my 1-B class. I was too busy to do it last night. I'm sorry about Frank, Melissa. Were you going to marry him?"

"No."

"Why not?"

"He wasn't very grown up—I mean, in the head. He used to quote me poetry—Herrick and Lovelace and that sort of stuff."

"They're good poets."

Melissa shrugged. "They're more in the Aldriches' style. You know, they're sort of an interesting pair. They're identical siblings. That's why they talk and even think alike. It seems that the one fertilized gene splits—"

"Pah!" said Beulah Porter Cowys. "That's Shirley Parker and her Freudian interpretation of biology again. I can recognize her touch. The Aldriches talk and think alike because they've lived within arm's reach of each other for sixty years, and that's the only reason. I'll see you later, Melissa. Keep your chin up."

She walked down the steps, and Carstairs leaned over and growled confidentially in Melissa's ear.

"What do you want?" Melissa demanded.

Carstairs licked his chops.

"Oh, dear," said Melissa. "Do I have to feed you, too? What on earth do you eat for breakfast? Orange juice, oatmeal, bacon and eggs?"

Carstairs tilted his head back and bayed joyously.

"Stop that!" Melissa ordered. "You'll wake up the whole

town! Can't you wait until I finish this cigarette? . . . Stop it, I
said! I'll feed you . . . Yes, right now. Come on."

CHAPTER THREE

THE STUDENTS WERE BEGINNING TO stir when Mel-
issa walked diagonally across the Old Quad with Carstairs tagging dutifully along behind her. The students gathered in cack-
ling flocks or walked alone brooding upon the pitfalls in aca-
demic life, as is their wont. Strangers are apt to be disconcerted
by their odd mannerisms, but Melissa was accustomed to them
and knew that all they needed was to be ignored.

Eric Trent was sitting on the front steps of Old Chem. He
stood up quickly when he saw Melissa and Carstairs and then,
realizing that they had already seen him, sat down again reluctantly and stared into space.

"Hello," said Melissa.,

"How do you do," Trent said warily.

"I'm tired," Melissa told him. "Will it distress you if I sit
here on the steps?"

"Not at all," said Trent.

Carstairs sat down, too, and regarded Trent in a speculative
way. He received no signs of recognition in return, and after a
moment he snorted once, loudly, and then lay down and went to
sleep.

There was a prolonged and weighty silence, and then finally
Trent said:

"I'm very sorry about last night. About your own experience,
and about the death of your friend."

"Thanks," said Melissa.

"In regard to your apartment. Doan spoke to my wife about
getting a larger one. He has to sleep on my chesterfield, and he
says it gives him bad dreams. My wife knows T. Ballard
Bestwyck. She arranged things with him. I had nothing to do

with it at all. I didn't know anything about it. Of course, I'm not going to appropriate your apartment. Doan can get himself a hotel room if he doesn't like my chesterfield."

"That's very sweet of you, sweet and generous," Melissa said and she looked at him with eyes that shone. "Maybe you aren't a bad guy after all—that is, not as much of a dope as I believed you to be at first after reading those sticky-icky things your wife said about you in her advertisements . . . However, before I can be sure, I'd like proof."

"What kind of proof?"

"Proof of how really sweet and generous you are. For instance, if you gave me back my office as well as my apartment, then I could believe some very fine things of you—practically any fine thing you wanted me to believe."

Trent regarded her with a puzzled frown. There was guile in her face but there was also sincerity. "Well," he said in a relenting tone. "Well . . ." But then he stopped relenting and lifted his chin with the air of a man who's been taken in by a female before and has no intention of being a two-time sucker. "No," he said firmly. "You don't need that particular office and I do."

"Hmmph," said Melissa, "so that's the way it is. And I'll bet I know why. You think Doan would figure you for a sissy if you gave in to a woman."

"That's not so."

"It is too. I know it is. Why do you put up with Doan, anyway? I mean, tagging you around and sleeping on your chesterfield and all that?"

"There's no way I could prevent him from following me around. There's no law against it. So I thought I might as well make the best of it. As a matter of fact, I like Doan. He's very good company. He's very adaptable. If I want to talk, he listens. If I want to study or work or read, he goes to sleep. Apparently he can sleep anytime, anywhere. Of course, there's always Carstairs. He's a bore."

Carstairs mumbled to himself.

"Why don't you assert yourself?" Melissa asked. "I mean,

why don't you tell Doan you'll sock him in the eye if he doesn't go away?"

Trent looked at her. "Doan? That wouldn't have the slightest effect. He's not afraid of violence at all. In fact, I think he enjoys it. I think that's why Carstairs likes him. Everyone else is afraid of Carstairs—at least, a little. Doan is not—not a bit."

"Well, they're rather odd chaperones. I should think they'd cramp your style."

"They don't. I'm not interested in women."

"Is that a fact?" said Melissa.

"Yes."

"Oh."

A shaky voice said, "P-p-please . . ."

Trent and Melissa looked up. There was a girl standing on the walk in front of the steps, facing them. She was wearing a plaid skirt and a red sweater, both turned inside out. She was wearing her left shoe on her right foot and her right shoe on her left foot. There was a circle painted in lipstick on one of her cheeks and a double cross drawn with eyebrow pencil on the other. Her hair was drawn right straight up from her head into a topknot and stiffened with soap or grease. She was holding a magazine in one hand and a fountain pen in the other.

"Please," she said, staring at Trent with dilated eyes, "will you autograph this—this for me?"

She held out the magazine open to one of the Heloise of Hollywood ads.

"What?" said Trent.

"Oh, please," said the girl. "If you don't, they'll take me back to the house and paddle me on my b-bare skin. And they paddle awfully hard."

"Who?" said Trent incredulously.

The girl rolled her eyes mutely to indicate a group of girls standing about twenty yards away. These were all normally dressed—that is, normally for girl students. They were watching with a sort of sly, breathless anticipation.

"What's the meaning of this?" Trent demanded.

"She's a pledge," said Melissa. "This is Hell Week for sorority pledges. She's going through her initiation. They always make pledges do embarrassing things like this—or worse. Let's see your pledge pin . . . She's a Delta Gamma. Go ahead and sign her ad. She really will get paddled unless you do."

"All right," said Trent.

The girl handed him the pen and the magazine. "Will you," she said, cringing, "will you sign it Handsome Lover Boy?"

Trent made a strangling noise.

"Oh, go ahead," Melissa said. "Give her a break."

Trent was white around the nostrils, but he signed.

"Aw, creepers," said the girl, breathing again. "Thanks a million, and I'm sorry."

Trent handed her the magazine and the pen. "Are any of your cute sorority sisters—any of the upperclassmen—taking meteorology?"

"Why, yes," said the girl. "Four or five of them."

"Tell them," said Trent, "not to bother about studying or turning in any papers I assign, because every one of them is going to flunk the course."

"You mean it?" said the girl. "Oh, good—good!"

She ran back to the group of girls. They opened up to receive her, giggling. The girl said something. The group stopped giggling. Their heads turned in unison in Trent's direction. They huddled and argued. They looked at Trent again. They turned around and walked away very soberly. The pledge, trailing behind, looked over her shoulder and leered gleefully.

"You cooled them off," said Melissa. "That house has been up before the Dean of Women once already this year for lousy grades. Are you really going to flunk them?"

"Yes."

"They'll send a delegation of seniors to apologize to you tomorrow."

"They'll still flunk."

"They'll wail at the Dean of Women and probably at T. Ballard Bestwyck."

"And they'll still flunk."

"You're sort of a determined character," said Melissa. "And awfully touchy."

"You're entitled to think so, if you like."

"Now don't get mad," Melissa said. "I know it's none of my business, but you can't blame me for being curious."

"What about?"

"Well, you act sometimes like you have half-good sense. You certainly knew what anyone intelligent would think about those ads. Why did you let your wife put them in all those magazines in the first place?"

"I didn't let her. I didn't know she was doing it."

"You can read, can't you?"

Trent looked at her, exasperated. "For the last four years— up until a few months ago—I was sitting on an ice pack in the middle of the Arctic Ocean. All my supplies and mail were delivered by jeep plane. I didn't order any women's magazines, and consequently I never saw one."

"What on earth were you doing in the middle of the Arctic Ocean?"

"That's where the weather makes up—the weather that affects the flying conditions on the Great Circle route through Alaska and Siberia. There were quite a few isolated weather stations up around there."

"Oh. Who was up there with you?"

"One Aleut and two Eskimos."

"Males?"

"Yes."

"I'm an anthropologist," Melissa said. "I know what they use to cure the furs they wear. Did these use it?"

"Yes."

"Ugh," said Melissa. "They must have been very sweet-smelling companions. I had the idea that you'd only been married about two years."

"That's right."

"Well, how *did* you manage it?"

"Do you know where Point Barrow is—on the extreme northern tip of Alaska?"

"I know now."

"Well, I came south to there from my station, in the supply plane, to get a tooth filled. There was a Navy port authority at the Point, and a Navy dentist called on them once in awhile. Heloise—my wife—was there at the time."

"What? What was she doing clear up there?"

"It seems that in her cosmetics she uses some very exotic materials of one sort and another. The juices from arctic lichen and moss and walrus blubber and all that sort of thing. This stuff was collected at Point Barrow. She had a big batch of it there, then. It was worth a lot of money, and the naval port commander refused to assign shipping space for it. She got passage on a transport plane—she has a great deal of influence—and went up to see about the matter. She was still arguing with the commander when I arrived."

"I see," said Melissa. "How many white women were living at Point Barrow?"

"At this time she was the only one there."

"Hmmm," said Melissa. "You'd been up on that ice floe for two years before that?"

"Yes."

"I see," said Melissa slowly.

"See what?"

"Oh, nothing. Just a little matter I was curious about."

"Heloise is a very attractive-looking woman."

"Did I say she wasn't? Is she actually fifty-four?"

"She doesn't look it."

"Not, anyway, after two years on an ice pack."

"That had nothing whatsoever to do with it!"

"Well, all right. Don't be so huffy. I'm not arguing with you."

"What are you doing?"

"Poking my nose in your business," Melissa admitted frankly. "You can snub me now, if you like."

"I can't snub everybody in the world."

"That's true enough. Can I ask you something else?"

"I don't know of any way I can stop you."

"Well," said Melissa, "isn't it true that when you got back here again and found out about those ads and sort of surveyed the rest of the feminine population—"

"No!"

"You don't even know what I was going to ask."

"I certainly do."

"Well, I'm not blaming you."

"Blaming me for what?"

"For getting smart and walking out on her."

"I didn't!"

"Oh, phooey," said Melissa. "She agreed to let you go peacefully if you'd lay low and let Doan keep tabs on you until she buried that Handsome Lover Boy drool and started another advertising campaign."

"You know," said Trent, "judging from your unconventional visitor last night, I should think you'd have enough troubles of your own to sort of keep you busy."

"I guess you're right," Melissa admitted. "What happened after I ran you out of my apartment last night?"

"Nothing, actually. I mean, they didn't find out anything except what Doan had already guessed. That Humphrey is so interested in getting something—it doesn't matter what, apparently—on Doan that he hardly has time for anything else. They went up to my apartment last night, and he and Doan both got drunk. The only change that rings in is that they argue more loudly. If you know who that prowler is, you're the only one who does or is likely to find out."

"Doan called your wife, didn't he? When he thought Humphrey would be likely to arrest him?"

"Yes."

"She must really know a lot of influential men in these parts."

"No. She knows their wives. You've seen that enormous monstrosity of a beauty salon of hers out on Sunset Boulevard, haven't you? Her headquarters? That place is staffed like a battleship.

She doesn't make any money out of it—even though the prices are something terrific. She keeps it for prestige. She lures motion picture stars into the place and fills them up with liquor—it's easy to get drunk in a steam cabinet—and then finagles free testimonials out of them."

"I don't think I'd like her."

"Nobody—I mean, perhaps not."

"I'd like to meet her, though."

Trent said, "If you ever do—and tell her that you know me—you're likely to get a reception that will surprise you."

"Why?" Melissa asked.

"Never mind. Just don't tell her."

A new voice said, "Hi, Melissa."

"Hello, Shirley," Melissa said.

This girl was small and slim and dark, dainty as a new doll. She had very large, mildly vague brown eyes and black hair gathered into two thick braids that dangled forward over her shoulders and down over an attractively prominent chest. She was wearing a sloppy-joe sweater with the sleeves pushed up and moccasins and a pair of blue denim jeans with three fountain pens in the right hip pocket.

"You look, terrible," she said to Melissa. "I heard about your prowler from Beulah Porter Cowys. That must have been a very interesting experience."

"Oh, it was."

"How did it make you feel? Now don't just tell me you were scared. I want to know specifically. Did you feel a tingling sensation in—"

"Shirley! Now, stop it! I didn't feel any tinglings, and I'm not going to talk about it any more."

"Well, why not?"

"Just because," said Melissa flatly and finally. "Shirley, this is Eric Trent—meteorology. This is Shirley Parker. She's a special—doing graduate work for a master's in psychology."

"How do you do," said Trent.

"You're Handsome Lover Boy," said Shirley.

"And what if I am?"

Shirley shrugged. "Now there's no point in reacting toward me in a hostile manner. The name is simply a word association picture with me. I don't feel any contempt toward you on account of it."

"Well, thanks very much," said Trent.

"Your attitude shows an obvious repression there. You ought to work it out. How do you feel when you approach your wife?"

"What?"

"You heard what I said. Wasn't the question clear?"

"It's clear that it's none of your business!"

"Oh, yes, it is. I'm writing a monograph on the subject—to get my master's. It's going to be published by the university press."

"I don't care to be in it."

"I wouldn't use your real name," Shirley assured him. "You'd just be an anonymous case history."

"No, thanks," said Trent.

"You're not showing the scientific attitude."

"You're right," Trent agreed.

"People make things very difficult for me," Shirley complained. "I mean, they're all so stupidly touchy on the subject of sex."

"Hi, everybody," said Doan. He was wearing a brown tweed sport coat now and brown tweed slacks and a dark green sport shirt.

"Hello, Mr. Doan," said Melissa.

"How do you feel this morning?" Trent asked.

"Not too bad," Doan told him. "I mean, I'm breathing—I think."

"Two of our third floor neighbors complained this morning about the noise last night."

"Humphrey always talks loud when he's drunk."

"You were doing all right in that line yourself."

"Self-defense," said Doan. "You have to talk loud to Humphrey, or else he won't pay any attention."

"He didn't, anyway."

Doan nodded. "Humphrey is very stupid, I fear. Who's this, here?"

Melissa said: "Shirley, this is Mr. Doan. He's a detective. This is Shirley Parker, Mr. Doan."

"You're cuter than a bug's ear," said Doan.

"I know it," said Shirley.

"She's writing a monograph," Eric Trent warned. "On sex."

"No," Shirley corrected. "Sex comes into it just incidentally. It's on psychotherapy. Psychosomatic therapy."

"That's nice," said Doan. "I bet."

"Do you have a sex life?" Shirley asked.

"Sure," said Doan. "But it's private."

"That's the way everyone acts," Shirley said. She stared at Carstairs in a speculative way. "What about him?"

"He does very well," said Doan. "He's different from most males. He gets paid for his services, and they're very much in demand. The owners of lady Great Danes have to write months ahead to get an appointment with him."

"Would you mind changing the subject?" Trent asked.

"Why?" Doan asked. "Sex is very interesting, and personally I think it's here to stay."

"Hallo, peoples," said Morales, coming out of the front door of Old Chem and shaking the dust from a mop gently over them all. "Nice day, no? Yes?"

"Did you paint my office?" Melissa demanded.

"Señorita, I have eight—"

"Yes, I know. Just forget it."

"Señorita, if you had eight children, you would know that forgetting them is difficult—not to say, impossible. Ah! And how do you do, Señorita Shirley?"

"Hello," said Shirley.

"Señorita Shirley, last night I had a very surprising experience."

"I don't want to hear about it."

"Señorita, this is a matter of immense scientific interest."

"How do you know?"

"Señorita, when a man has eight children, he acquires a certain flair in this field which gives him superior judgment."

"I'm not interested," Shirley told him.

"Señorita, in my opinion you are discriminating against me. I would bear it in silence, except for the fact that my experiences are of enormous scientific value. Just regard the matter objectively, Señorita. Incorporated in your book, my unparalleled performances would make your reputation."

"No doubt," said Shirley. "But they're not going to be—incorporated in my monograph, I mean. You're too disgustingly normal."

"Señorita, I resent that."

"Go ahead and resent."

Morales glowered darkly. "There is very little justice in this world, in my opinion." He hitched the mop up over his shoulder and marched back inside the building.

Shirley looked at Doan. "Did you ever kill anyone? I mean, either indirectly—by getting them hung, or directly—by doing your own dirty work?"

"Both ways," Doan answered.

"Do you rationalize your sadism when you do? I mean, in the manner judges do—by claiming they are ridding society of a menace and all that stuff?"

"No," said Doan. "I do it because I get paid for it. It's nice work."

"I'm afraid you're normal, too."

"I'm sorry," Doan told her.

"Do you know many murderers?"

"Hundreds."

"Are they paranoid or cycloid? It's my opinion that all of them are paranoid to some degree."

"What does that mean?"

"They're paranoiacs," Shirley explained. "It means they live in a subjective world of their own. They rationalize their destructive impulses by a cockeyed logic that has no relation to reality. Hitler was a marvelous one."

"I've never met a murderer who went in for it on such a big scale as he did," Doan said. "Although I did run across a nice old female party who knocked oft twenty people with nicotine distilled from bug spray."

"Were her victims all of one sex?"

"Nope. Men, women, and children. She wasn't a bit choosy."

Shirley nodded indifferently. "Generalized transference of a subconscious repressed aggression. It's very common. Well, I'm going in and try to get something out of Professor Sley-Mynick."

"Oh, Shirley," said Melissa. "Leave him alone. You know you terrify the poor man with your questions so much you make him ill."

"It's good for him," said Shirley. "He's got to work out those experiences—get them up and out in the open. He'll never get well if he keeps them seething in his subconscious the way they are."

A fat shadow waddled out from the doorway and on emerging into the sunlight turned out to be Professor Sley-Mynick himself. He blinked behind his heavy glasses and then, settling his gaze on the group standing and sitting on the steps, twisted around suddenly and looked as though he was going to scurry back from where he'd come.

"Just a minute, Professor," Shirley Parker called to him. "You're the very man I want to see. We were talking about abnormal psychology—about murderers and. . ."

The professor threw up his hands. "Oh, dear," he said. "Did you say murderers? Who's a murderer? I'm not a murderer, am I? I don't know any murderer. Or do I?"

Shirley tripped up the steps and patted Sley-Mynick on the shoulder. "Now don't be alarmed," she told him, "Our discussion was purely objective, no personalities involved. We were talking about murderers and sex. As you know, I'm writing a monograph and in order to do it I have to interview people and get material on their sex experiences. I wanted to ask you . . ."

If the professor had seemed startled before, now he looked positively horrified. "Oh, dear," he said. "Sex. Do I have any sex? What sex am I? Male, of course. And you're a female. . . Oh, dear!"

The poor man retreated back into the building. Shirley had a grip on his elbow now and she dragged along after him until they were both out of sight in the lobby.

"She's pretty, isn't she?" Melissa asked.

"And how," Doan agreed. "Is she married?"

"Shirley? No. She doesn't believe in marriage."

"Is she a communist?" Trent asked warily.

Melissa laughed. "Of course not. Shirley wouldn't go in for anything as old hat as that. She's a philosophical anarchist."

"Oh," said Trent. "Well, excuse me. I have a ten o'clock class." He looked to make sure Shirley was not in sight in the hall and then went in and up the stairs.

"You know," Melissa said to Doan, "he's not so bad, after all. I mean, I thought he'd be an awfully icky sort of a wolf until I got his side of the story. He's sort of cute and innocent, isn't he?"

"Well," said Doan, "I suppose that all depends on your point of view. Don't let his face fool you. He gets mad quick, and when he does it's not a good idea to be standing around within arm's reach of him. He's a judo expert among other things, and he's hard as nails. Since I've been following him around, he has put away about twenty characters who made cracks of one sort or another to him about those Heloise ads, and so far he hasn't even gotten his hair mussed. I talk soft and smile loud with him. I don't want him mad at me. Even Carstairs detours around him."

"That reminds me," said Melissa. "Thank you just oodles for letting Carstairs stay with me."

"What did he do?" Doan inquired.

"It would take two hours to tell you, but right now you can have him back''

"Look," said Doan seriously, "I know he's a pest, but I think you'd better keep him with you. He does have sense enough to guard you."

Carstairs stood up. He looked levelly and coldly at Melissa and then at Doan. After he had done that, he went down the steps and along the walk about twenty paces—just out of earshot— and lay down on the grass.

"It irritates him to have people discuss him," Doan explained, "because he can't talk back—thank God. You'd better let him follow you around."

"Well, why?"

"Look," said Doan. "There was a prowler in your apartment last night. Remember?"

"That was just an accident. I mean, that he was in my apartment."

"Do you think Frank Ames cut his own throat by accident?"

Melissa shivered.

"That's more like it," said Doan. "That bird was no hallucination, and he's no joke. He carries both a knife and a gun, and last night wasn't the first time he's used them."

"Who do you think he was?"

"I don't know. Do you?"

"No!"

"Think back," Doan requested. "Think of the way he looked— the way he moved. Have you got a mental picture?"

"Y-yes."

"Could it have been a woman?"

"What?" said Melissa, staring.

"Humphrey had a hunch in that direction, and sometimes— by sheer accident—he gets a grip on an idea that makes sense. Do you think this prowler could have been a woman dressed up as a man?"

Melissa felt her jaw. "No."

"That blow doesn't mean anything either way. Some women can hit mighty hard. It's just a matter of knowing how, not of strength. Keep thinking. Was there anything off-center or unusual about this party?"

"Well," said Melissa, trying. "Well . . ."

"Go ahead."

"Nothing I can put my finger on. But something about the way he moved . . . Something queer and strange and yet horribly familiar. . . Something sort of out-of-focus. . ."

"How well do you know Beulah Porter Cowys?"

"Oh, don't be ridiculous!"

"I'm not," said Doan. "I'm worried. I tell you, this is a very bad boy we're dealing with. He's got lots of confidence. He uses a .22, which is a very light gun, but it really doesn't matter how big a hole you get punched in you if it's in a vulnerable place. Last night he was shooting in the dark—he couldn't see his sights—and he couldn't have seen more of me than just a blur, and he shot awfully fast, but even at that he would have hit me all three times if I hadn't moved in the wrong direction at just the right time. I'd hate to meet him when he could see well."

"You're scaring me now."

"I'm trying to. Think back again. What was he doing when you first saw him?"

"It sounds silly, but he was looking at a pair of my stockings as though he'd never seen any before."

"He didn't take anything?"

"No."

"What else did he disturb—besides your bureau or dresser or whatever?"

"Nothing. Just that one drawer."

"Yeah," said Doan absently.

"Are you really considering Beulah as a suspect?"

Doan frowned. "I don't see how it could have been her. She had the time, all right. You were still unconscious when she turned up, and Trent thinks it was about seven or eight minutes after I started chasing. But he was so busy dithering around over you it might have been an hour for all he'd know. I made some experiments. In her apartment, with the door closed,, it would be hard to hear a fire siren in your apartment. None of the other tenants heard you. We did because your door was open, and the hall funnels the sound. But if Beulah Porter Cowys has a stocking mask around, she's carrying it with her. Along with an automatic and a knife, and that doesn't seem reasonable. She does have a pair of black leather gloves, though."

"Did you search her apartment?"

"Sure."

"How'd you get in?"

"The locks in that building are easy to pick. Of course, too, she could have circled around and gone in the front of the building after she shot at me—it's physically possible—but I don't believe she could have done it without Carstairs spotting her."

"Why don't you let Carstairs just sniff around until he locates whoever it was?"

"Carstairs?" Doan said. "He's not that kind of a dog. He can't smell any better than I can. He operates with his ears and his eyes."

"Look here," said Melissa. "Why are you so interested in me and in my prowler?"

"Why, Melissa," Doan chided. "I love you. Did I forget to tell you?"

"Pooh," said Melissa. "We can't use that. Come on. I've cooperated. Now, give."

Doan said slowly, "I noticed something I don't think Humphrey spotted. You know that directory in the lobby of the Pavilion? The one that lists the names of the tenants opposite the number of the apartment each lives in? Well, the manager or someone had already put Trent's name opposite your apartment and yours opposite Trent's last night. You know, because Trent insists on exchanging apartments with you and—"

"I know all about who wants to exchange apartments and why."

"Oh," said Doan. "Well, that chesterfield in Trent's apartment is too damned short. Now if you'd just let me sleep in that pull-down bed in your living room . . ."

"I wouldn't care for that arrangement."

"Okay," said Doan.

"Just a minute here!" said Melissa. "Don't try to get off the subject. You're so concerned about this because you think—on account of the directory—that the prowler made a mistake in the apartments. You think he intended to get into Trent's apartment instead of mine!"

"Yes," Doan admitted. "And I think that's why he was staring at your stockings in such a dumbfounded way when you came in, he naturally didn't expect to find a drawer full of women's stuff in Trent's apartment."

"Well, what do you think he did expect to find?"

"I don't know. That's what I'm worried about. This bird is no ordinary prowler—no garden variety of sneak thief. And anyway, Trent has no dough, aside from a big gob of back Navy pay which is in the bank. He hasn't any rajah's rubies or any secret plans for atomic bombs. I can't figure out what the prowler was after, and why he was willing to go to such lengths to keep from being caught. I mean, look at it this way. Suppose I had caught him—or rather, suppose Frank Ames had. The prowler hadn't stolen a thing. All he could possibly have drawn would be a couple of years for breaking and entering. And yet, he was willing—and ready to commit murder to dodge that. It doesn't make sense."

"So you think it was a woman."

Doan grinned. "Not for that reason. But sometimes they do funny things when they get bitten by the love bug, and Trent is dynamite in that direction."

"Oh-*ho!*" said Melissa suddenly,

"What now?" Doan demanded warily.

"I'm just getting the drift of all these sly, snide questions of yours. I know who you're eyeing."

"Just relax, now," Doan advised.

"I won't. You're thinking about somebody whose name starts with H and who hangs around in Hollywood."

"There's still a law against slander," Doan warned.

"Pooh. No wonder you're worried. You're afraid you might be guarding Trent against your own boss."

"You've got an evil mind, Melissa," Doan told her.

"Haven't I, just? But it works, doesn't it? So Heloise is a crack shot with a pistol, is she?"

"I don't know," said Doan, "but she used to juggle knives."

"She did? Really? Where?"

"In carnivals and at county fairs."

"How do you know?"

"I investigated her. I always investigate the people who hire me. I want to know whether their checks are good."

"She must have millions!"

"Maybe, now," Doan said. "But back in the thirties there was a time when she was on the ropes financially. Her outfit nearly foundered under her."

"What happened?"

"Her husband forged her name and misused a limited power of attorney to dribble all her assets into the stock market."

"Her *husband?* You mean, another one? Has she been married before?"

"Oh, yes. To a guy named 'Big Tub' Tremaine. He was a spieler on a sick pitch."

"What does that mean?"

"He sold medicines at carnivals and fairs—Kickapoo Joy Juice and Colonel Ouster's Calibrated Cure-All and stuff like that. Heloise was his come-on. She used to dress in spangled diapers and a necklace and juggle knives to attract a crowd so Big Tub could work them over. He was good at it, from all accounts."

"What happened to him?"

"He died."

"Ah-ha," said Melissa. "Mysteriously, I'll bet."

"Nope. He dunked himself in the drink of his own free will and accord—and right in front of about a hundred witnesses who were all chasing him to stop him."

"Why did he do that? Kill himself, I mean?"

"Because he was smart," said Doan. "He stole money from Heloise. That's just about as serious an offense as there is. If she could have laid hands on him she'd have had him boiled in oil or, at the very least, drawn and quartered.

"Have you ever heard about the other guy who stole money from Heloise?"

"No," said Melissa, "I haven't heard. Tell me about the other guy."

"I've forgotten his name but he worked for her as a book-keeper. He figured out a complicated and what he thought was a foolproof system for rigging the books. He'd embezzled the magnificent sum of one dollar and seventy-six cents when she got wise to him. He was bonded and Heloise forced the bonding company to prosecute, although they didn't want to. The court, however, threw the case out. They said stealing a dollar seventy-six was hardly a misdemeanor, much less a felony. Whereupon, Heloise decided to prosecute in her own way—not through the courts . . ."

"Did she fire the fellow?"

"No, she kept him on—raised his salary, in fact, so high that the poor guy's wife wouldn't let him quit. Heloise wanted him right under her thumb where she could torture him. But she didn't let him keep books any longer. She made him the manager of her complaint department, and if you want to live a life of hell and damnation just go get yourself a job in the complaint department of a cosmetics manufacturer."

"I can imagine," said Melissa.

"I wonder if you can," Doan told her. "This poor ex-book-keeper, with the sensitive soul you'll find in most embezzlers, had to take lip from women all over the United States and some foreign countries who'd bought Heloise of Hollywood's beauty preparations and hadn't turned out as beautiful as the advertisements said they would. They stormed the poor guy by letter, telegram, telephone and in person. All of them were mad, some of them madder. His nerves gave out."

"What finally happened to him?"

"He went off his bat, which is what Heloise had counted on. They've got him stuck away now in a nuthouse somewhere in a room wallpapered with mattresses. The doctors say he'll never get any better."

"Ugh," said Melissa. "This Heloise must be plenty tough."

"She is that," said Doan, "but a good businesswoman. She

built up her business all on her own, although she did and does use the sap bait Big Tub taught her. He had nothing to do with the management of it. She supported him in relative luxury until he started giving her money to the stockbrokers."

"Where did he kill himself?"

"At Ensenada. He dove off a fishing pier after loading himself down with most of the liquor in the nearest bar and bidding all the patrons a fond farewell. They just thought he was crocked, until he actually did heave himself overboard, and then they had a hell of a time fishing him out again. When they did, he was deader than a kippered herring."

"I'd really like to see Heloise," Melissa said ruminatively. "I mean, in person. She interests me."

"Is that a fact?" Doan inquired politely. "Heloise interests you?"

"Don't get funny."

"You'd better forget Trent. He's out of your league."

"Oh, is that so?"

"I'm just telling you," Doan said. "I'm your friend."

"Ha!"

"Now just think. Suppose by some freak of chance you did manage to land him. He looks just as good to other gals as he does to you, remember."

"I could handle that angle, all right. And without hiring a detective to watch him. Does Heloise give her personal attention to that salon of hers on the Strip?"

"Yes," Doan admitted. "But if I were you, I wouldn't show up around there."

"I will if I please, and I think I please."

"Well, take Carstairs with you, anyway."

"I can't. I haven't a car. It's against the law for dogs to ride on buses."

"Let him handle that situation. I've never yet run across a bus driver who could keep him off a bus or put him off once he got on . . . Carstairs!"

Carstairs raised his head languidly.

"Go with her," said Doan. "Watch it."

Carstairs lifted his upper lip and sneered at hint in an elaborately bored way.

CHAPTER FOUR

THE SUNSET STRIP IS A SECTION OF THE county, not incorporated into the city of Los Angeles, which points like an accusing finger directly at the heart of Hollywood. It is inhabited by actors and actresses and their exploiters or victims, and by people who have been run out of Beverly Hills, and by bookmakers, saloon keepers, unsuccessful swindlers, antique dealers and interior decorators of one kind or the other, but mostly the other. It is considered quite fascinating by the sort of people who like to go on bus rides through the Bowery.

Heloise of Hollywood had a building all of her own in the center of this streamlined slum. The building featured glass brick and chrome and pink plaster and dainty gestures in the air, and taken over all it was as slick and as screwy as one of Salvador Dali's copyrighted hallucinations.

There had been a certain amount of opposition to Carstairs' presence on the bus, and Melissa was feeling a little frazzled out when she went up the steps and pushed open the pink, padded door that was billed as "The Pathway to Perfection—Entrance."

"Well, for goodness' sakes, come on," she said impatiently.

Carstairs ambled up the steps and looked inside. He grunted, and the hair stood up on his back.

Melissa kicked him. "Go on!"

Carstairs went in reluctantly. Melissa followed him, and her hair stood up, too.

The foyer was a passageway about five miles long and lined with mirrors. These weren't distortion mirrors—not quite. They were just very, very clear and brilliantly lighted, and they magnified matters just enough. Melissa watched herself walk, because there was nothing else she could do. She saw herself highlighted from fore to aft and from top to bottom and from some other odd and interesting angles. It was the most sadistically efficient sales promotion for beauty treatments she had ever run across.

Even Carstairs had begun to cringe by the time he had reached the mirror door at the end. Melissa held it open for him, and they entered a plush-lined cubicle which featured a tall, round ebony desk placed in its exact center. There was a girl behind the desk, and she was beautiful. She really was. She had black, glistening hair and a corpse-like pallor and a face so perfectly contoured it was frightening.

Women who look like this usually sound like crows, but this one had been trained. Her voice was soft and insinuatingly confidential.

"How do you do?" she said, as though she were actually interested. "May I help you?"

"I think so," said Melissa. "Can you do something about my cheek?"

"Your cheek?"

"Yes. Right here. My husband beat me last night."

"Of course. Do you wish it to look worse or better?"

"What?" said Melissa.

The girl smiled at her. "Those incidents happen so rarely to some of our more unfortunate clients that they often wish to capitalize on them when they do."

"Capitalize?" Melissa repeated.

The girl moved her right hand casually, and the big diamond on her fourth finger sparkled.

"Oh," said Melissa. "No. I want it to look better. It always irritates my boyfriend when my husband beats me, and I want the two of them to stay pals."

"Naturally. May I have your name?"

"Susan Halfinger."

"And who is sponsoring you?"

"Sponsoring? Oh. T. Ballard Bestwyck. He's the president of—"

"Oh, we know T. Ballard here."

"You do?" Melissa said, startled. "Oh, of course. His wife."

"Wife?" said the girl, just as startled. "Oh, yes. Yes, indeed. His wife."

"Hmmm," said Melissa thoughtfully. .

"Would your dog like something to play with while he is waiting? We have some very enchanting rubber mice that squeak."

"No," Melissa said judicially. "I don't believe he'd care for that sort of thing."

"Then if you'll just step into the anteroom . . .Through that door . . .Yes . . .Our bruise specialist will be prepared for you in just a few short moments."

"Thanks," said Melissa.

She opened the door and ushered Carstairs through it into a long, narrow room cluttered with dusty pink lounges with scrolled gilt legs.

There were three fat women sitting in a row on one of the lounges. The nearest one bounced up and down and pointed a pudgy, admiring finger at Carstairs.

"Ooooh! Look!"

The middle one patted her hands and cooed.

"Darling!" said the third one. "Just delicious!"

Carstairs backed up against Melissa. Melissa pushed him away and sat down on one of the lounges. Carstairs crept up and huddled against her legs.

"He's so pretty!" said the nearest fat one.

"Ippy-ippy-ippy-tweeeeet," said the middle one.

"Those divine brown eyes," said the third one.

Carstairs moaned in a soft, terrified way.

Another door opened, and a girl looked in. This one was a cool tall blonde. She was dressed in a white uniform, but it was white silk, and it had been made just for her. She looked like nurses should look but never do.

"Miss Halfinger," she said. She waited for a moment and then said more pointedly: "Miss Halfinger."

"Eh?" said Melissa. "Oh! Yes."

She got up and started for the door. Carstairs started right after her.

"You stay here," Melissa ordered.

Carstairs stared at her in incredulous dismay.

"Lie down," Melissa said. "Wait."

Carstairs whimpered piteously.

Melissa stamped her foot. "Lie *down!*"

Carstairs began to fold himself up reluctantly.

"Ippy-ippy," cooed the middle fat one.

"Just too precious," said the third fat one.

Melissa closed the door and followed the blonde down a passageway that had dark brown cork flooring and beige walls and a yellow ceiling. Along each side, at staggered intervals, there were doors curtained with white oiled silk. From inside of the rooms came sharply distinct slaps, the grisly cracking of reluctant joints, retchings and gaggings and moans, and sobbing pleas for mercy.

Melissa and her guide turned a corner and went past a hideous place full of malignantly coiling serpents of steam vapor and pinkly parboiled things that squeaked and jibbered in their agony.

"Right in here," said the blonde, swishing aside one of the oiled silk curtains.

This wasn't a cubicle. It was as large as an ordinary hotel room. It contained a desk and a chair and a couch equipped with smelling salts and a telephone. It was as obtrusively antiseptic as an operating amphitheater.

"Just take off your clothes," said the blonde. "The shower is behind that door."

"What?" said Melissa. "Wait a minute. My husband fights fair. He just pasted me one. He didn't kick me after I was down."

"The Pathway to Perfection," said the blonde, "lies in the complete realignment of all the component parts of the body to express the poetry of true beauty."

"Okay," said Melissa.

"The towels are on the table. The water is electronized and energized. I will return."

"Do that," said Melissa.

She took off her clothes and put on a rubber bathing cap that came in a sealed cellophane container. She opened the frosted door the blonde had pointed out. The shower was about eight by eight, all black shiny tile, and was worked by a control panel as complicated as a transport plane's. Melissa twisted some knobs and turned others for a while and finally got the right combination. There were approximately one thousand water jets of varying capacity and intensity, and some of them apparently gave out with cologne instead of water.

Melissa walked right in and luxuriated. She stayed until she began to feel washed away and then came out and selected one of the towels. It was as big as a bed sheet and as fluffy as a cloud. Melissa was all tangled up in it when she heard the first scream.

She didn't pay any attention.

Immediately there were some more screams. They were very loud, very terrorized screams in different voices that blended in a sort of chromatic progression that was not unpleasing to the ear. Melissa stopped rubbing to listen. The screams kept mounting in volume and in pitch, and now there were some other noises—metallic clanging and the crash of shattered glass.

And through all this—as a sort of a minor undertone—something was howling. Melissa suddenly isolated that last sound and identified its source. She ducked out into the hall dragging the towel behind her.

The screams now were multitudinously deafening. They had begun to echo and meet each other in midair. The air began to quiver and palpitate.

Carstairs spun around the corner down the hall, leaning far over and scrabbling for his footing. His mouth was wide open, and he was making a lot of noise.

"Here!" said Melissa, waving the towel.

She wasn't wearing any clothes, and she still had her bathing cap on. She was just another naked woman. Carstairs wailed and skidded and hiked back around the corner. The screaming redoubled.

Melissa ran, trying frantically to wrap the towel around herself. She reached the corner. There were screams to her right and screams to her left and screams in front of her, undulating in weird concatenation. Their intensity seemed to center toward the left. Melissa went that way.

She turned into a long low room where sun lamps coiled like chromium cobras among women who screamed and squirmed and clutched at themselves. She ran through another room where women writhed helplessly in the metallic grip of permanent wave machines. She got out into another hall in time to see Carstairs hurdle gracefully over a pile of whooping casualties.

Melissa fought and clawed her way over cringing, sweaty bodies and made it out into the clear again. Carstairs had hit a dead end and was on his way back, running with desperate, driving effort.

"Stop, you!" Melissa shrieked. She swooped at him, arms spread.

Carstairs dodged and whipped sideways through a curtained doorway, and Melissa went right after him. It was a low-ceilinged, dank room with a white tiled floor and walls that glistened damply. Carstairs was headed for the door at the other end.

Right in front of this door there was an oblong opening in the floor—a little longer and a little wider than a grave. It was filled to the brim with something black and malignantly slick. Carstairs intended to jump over it. His foot slipped.

He yelled—one last, lorn note of utter despair. He fell full length in the mud bath, and the mud bath went off in an explosion that splattered the whole room and everything in it, including Melissa.

Carstairs was incapable of making any more noise, but he wasn't defeated, even now. He scrambled frantically to get out. Melissa wiped the mud out of her eyes and hit him with her fist in the approximate spot she judged his head was.

"Stop, stop!"

Carstairs couldn't stop. He got out of the mud bath, carrying most of its contents on him. He got out through the door, staggering, and bumbled down another hall with Melissa scrambling and grabbing behind him.

The door at the end of the hall was closed. Carstairs lunged and hit it with his remaining strength. The door popped open. Carstairs fell into the anteroom. The three fat ladies were long gone. Carstairs was trying feebly to crawl under one of the dusty pink lounges when Melissa landed on him.

"Carstairs!" she shouted furiously. She dug through the mud and found an ear and jerked it hard. "I'm me! I'm here!"

Carstairs blubbered at her in pitiable relief. He tried to sit in her lap.

Melissa punched him. "Behave yourself, you fool!" There were knees digging into her back, and Melissa brushed at them absently. "Get away and give me room to . . . What?" She turned her head slowly.

Eric Trent was sitting on the lounge. His mouth was open.

There was one of those silences.

Melissa suddenly remembered her towel. She pulled it up higher. That was bad. She pulled it down lower. That was not good, either.

"Turn around, you gaping idiot!" she snarled.

Trent behaved as though he hadn't heard her. There was a look on his face that was half a smile of amusement and half an expression of artistic appreciation. "Gosh, Melissa," he said, "you've got a pretty nice—er—you look pretty wonderful—er— what I mean is. . ."

"I know what you mean!" Melissa spat. "So this is what those years on an icicle or iceberg or whatever did to you, is it? Ogling helpless unclothed women!" She scraped a handful of mud off her thigh and hurled it at him. "Didn't you hear me? I said *turn your head!*"

A glob of mud struck Trent on the nose. He turned his head so fast his neck clicked.

Melissa rewound the towel. "All right," she told him.

Trent looked at her and swallowed. "Did you have an accident or—or something?"

"Me?" said Melissa. "Oh, no. I do this sort of thing all day every day."

Trent swallowed again. "I—see."

Melissa took off her bathing cap and slapped at him viciously with it. "Why do you always have to be sneaking around and spying on me?"

Trent blocked the blow with his arm. "I am not sneaking around and I am not spying on you."

"You liar. Doan told you I was coming here, so you had to come snooping."

"Doan didn't either tell me you were coming here. I had no idea you were."

"Pooh-bah! I suppose you came to get a permanent wave? You don't need it. The one you have hasn't grown out yet."

"I came here," said Trent evenly, "because my wife sent for me."

"That was very nice of you, Eric," said a new voice. It was a voice that was hoarsely hollow and smooth at the same time. It sounded a little like a billiard ball rolling down a rain spout.

Melissa turned her head slowly again.

This was Heloise of Hollywood. She was tall and erect and sleekly slim, and she had jade green eyes. There wasn't a line in her face or a wrinkle in her neck, but she was fifty-four years old. No one could possibly have gotten as hard as she was in less than that time. The hardness wasn't a mask—it wasn't even striated. It was smooth and icy from outside in and from inside out. She radiated as much warmth as a diamond.

She studied Melissa for a moment. "Is that your dog?"

"I'm responsible for him."

Heloise nodded. "I wondered if you'd lie—again."

"What do you mean by that?"

"Your name is Melissa Gregory—not Halfinger."

"My name is what I choose to call myself."

Heloise shrugged indifferently. "Quite. I know the dog. It belongs to Doan. It should be shot. It's mad, I think. It started on this rampage just because one of my more stupid customers, who was waiting in here, tried to tie a pink hair ribbon around its neck."

"That would make me mad, too."

Heloise studied her again and then looked at Trent. "I'm afraid your taste is deteriorating, my dear. She's a mess. Even her feet are dirty."

They were.

Trent wiped the mud off his nose with a finger and said: "I wouldn't go too far, if I were you, Heloise."

"Wouldn't you, Eric?" Heloise asked, idly interested.

"No."

They watched each other, and Melissa shivered.

The receptionist came in from the foyer. "Madame, there are two men outside."

"How very interesting," said Heloise.

"Both of them say they are detectives. They are handcuffed together."

"Send them in."

"Yes, Madame." The receptionist had really tried hard, but temptation overcame her. She rolled her eyes in Eric Trent's direction and twitched her hips at him.

In one smooth, deadly motion Heloise picked up a heavy crystal ashtray and threw it. The receptionist shut the door quickly. The ashtray made a dent in it and then clattered dully on the floor.

"Doan must be in trouble again," Heloise said casually.

Humphrey shouldered through the door, dragging Doan along behind him.

"Hi, everybody," Doan said amiably.

"Shut up," Humphrey ordered, jerking on the cuffs that fastened his left arm to Doan's right. "What's going on in this joint, anyway? I heard a lot of screaming."

"A couple of my customers got a little hysterical," Heloise told him.

"It sounded more like—" Humphrey stopped and stared incredulously. "Wheee-hooo! Look at that, will you? Wheee-hooo-

hooo-hooo!" He collapsed against the wall, shaking helplessly with laughter.

Heloise said impatiently: "Take the dog inside and clean it up. And you'd better do a little work on yourself at the same time."

Melissa groped through a crust of mud and located Carstairs' collar. She led him toward the inner door. When they reached it, Carstairs suddenly twitched the collar out of her grasp and turned around. His eyes were bright red.

Humphrey stopped laughing.

Carstairs turned around again and preceded Melissa through the door. Melissa slammed it emphatically behind her.

"Say," said Humphrey uneasily, "I didn't like the way he looked at me just then."

"You thought about that a little bit too late," Doan said. "Don't ever let him catch you up a dark alley. People who laugh at him often have fatal accidents."

"He caused plenty of accidents here," Heloise said. "He ran wild through this place. He must have damaged a thousand dollars worth of equipment."

"That was naughty of him," said Doan. "I shall speak to him severely."

"Not only that, but he caused a general attack of hysteria among the customers."

"Charge them for it."

Heloise stared at him. "You know, sometimes you act quite bright." She snapped her fingers.

The receptionist opened the door and looked around its edge cautiously. "Yes, Madame?"

"Double all the bills this afternoon."

"Yes, Madame."

In the back room one of the girls started the old screaming routine again.

Heloise's nostrils flared. "If that dog. . ."

The scream whooped down the corridor in their direction, and then the door of the anteroom burst open.

"Gad," said Humphrey in an awed murmur.

The screamer was pink and enormous and bare as the day she was born.

"Murder!" she squalled at them. *"Murr-durr!"*

She collapsed, then, in a suety quivering heap.

"Gad," said Humphrey, even more awed.

A white-clad attendant came down the hall carrying a sheet. She dropped the sheet over the screamer, and the sheet began to quiver uncannily, too.

"Madame," said the attendant, "there is a corpse in one of the massage rooms."

"What?" said Humphrey, suddenly coming to. "What was that?"

"Is it a customer?" Heloise asked.

"Yes, Madame."

"Hey!" said Humphrey. "Corpse? Did I hear you say— corpse?"

Heloise stepped over the quivering sheet and started down the corridor. "What number?"

"Seven, Madame."

"Here!" said Humphrey. He darted after Heloise, tugging Doan along in his wake.

Eric Trent got up from the lounge and followed them. Heloise went to the right at the first turn and to the right again and then stopped and pushed aside a white curtain.

It was a room similar to the one Melissa had used, except that in this one a long white rubbing table with gleaming tubular legs was fastened to the floor under the drop light in the center. There was a woman lying on the table completely covered with a massage sheet except for her bony, beaked face and her long, crook-toed feet. Her tongue was sticking out in a last sardonic gesture of defiance. She was laid out just as though she were in a morgue, and she was just as dead.

"It's the old scrawny dame!" Humphrey blurted. He jerked on the handcuffs. "What's her name?"

"Beulah Porter Cowys," said Doan.

Heloise stepped forward and pulled the sheet down a little. They could all see the spreading blue-black splotches on the lined throat.

"Strangled," said Eric Trent.

Humphrey shot out a pointed finger. "And you were here at the time! I've had an eye on you all the time, bub! You were afraid the old scrawny dame would squawk to your wife about you and that Melissa number, and so you followed her here and planted Doan outside for a lookout and sicked that damned Carstairs on the customers to create a riot, and then you wrung her neck for her!"

"What's your name?" Heloise asked coldly.

"Huh? Humphrey."

"He's the same one," said Doan.

Heloise walked over to the couch and picked up the telephone. "Get me the sheriff's office. His headquarters."

"That's not going to do you one bit of good," Humphrey informed her, "because this is a very clear-cut case of conspiracy to—"

Heloise spoke into the telephone: "Hello. This is Heloise of Hollywood. I want to speak to your boss. Hello, Mouthy? This is Heloise. I had some of my friends speak to you last night about one of your trained apes. He's here at my place now, annoying me. I'm getting a little tired of this character, Mouthy. I want you to talk to him. This time make things clear." She held out the phone toward Humphrey.

Humphrey took it gingerly. "Hello." The phone buzzed at him like a rattlesnake. "Yes, sir. But—Yes, sir . . . But I—Yes, sir. . .No, sir . . . But there's been another murder right here in— Yes, sir. . .Yes, sir . . . Yes, sir... Yes, sir . . . Yes, sir." The phone popped and quit rattling.

"Well?" said Heloise. "Have you got things straight now?"

"Yes, ma'am," said Humphrey soberly.

Two uniformed deputies from one of the sheriff's radio prowl cars shouldered into the room.

"Oh, hello," said one of them, recognizing Humphrey. "Some

dame phoned in and said there was a murder—"

"Shut up," said Humphrey. "Don't even mention the word. It's all a mistake. The dame, here, committed suicide."

"Huh?" said the deputy. "Suicide? She's got finger marks on her gullet."

"So she choked herself to death!" Humphrey snarled. "Is it any of your business? Do you want to disturb the customers? Beat it! Go home!"

The deputies backed off reluctantly. One said, "Well, we'll have to make a report . . ."

"Yeah," said Humphrey. "To the sheriff, and I want to be right there when you do. I want to hear that. I'm coming with you now."

He started down the hall.

Doan jerked him to a halt. "I don't want to walk around with you any more."

"You'll walk or get carried."

"Wait a minute," said Trent. "What did you arrest him for this time?"

"For loitering and suspicion of grand larceny—auto. He was loafing out in front in a car that wasn't his."

"That's my car," sand Trent, "and I told him to wait in it while I was in here."

"Take those handcuffs off him," said Heloise.

"Yes, ma'am," said Humphrey, obeying.

"Get out," said Heloise. "And stay out."

"Yes, ma'am," said Humphrey.

The shadows were stretching long and thin over the mathematical segments of lawn when Doan and Eric Trent walked diagonally across the Quad. They found Humphrey sitting and brooding on the front steps of Old Chem. He was hunched up, with his chin resting grimly in his hands. He looked like he had been sitting for quite some time and intended to keep on doing it until he got what he wanted.

"Look who's loitering now," Doan said.

"Shut up," said Humphrey. He was watching Trent. "What are you doing here? You've got no classes at this hour of the day."

"I don't think it's any of your business," Trent informed him, "but I don't mind telling you. I came over to take a sundown reading on my instruments."

"What instruments?"

"Various weather recording instruments. You wouldn't know what they were if I told you."

"What are you doing here?" Doan inquired.

Humphrey nodded at him. "You're a very clever lad, Doan."

"This is so sudden," said Doan.

"Yeah. You're clever, and you've got lots of heavy artillery in the shape of influence lined up behind you. But I'm clever, too."

"No kidding?" Doan asked, surprised.

"Yup. And I'm mad."

"Dear me," said Doan.

"And I've got an idea."

"Oh, boy."

"Do you want to hear it?"

"No."

"You're going to, though," said Humphrey. "My idea is this Melissa Gregory."

"Why don't you just relax for a while, Humphrey?"

"Shut up. Melissa Gregory is at the bottom of this pileup, and you're not going to lure me off on any of your false trails."

"I suppose she popped herself on the jaw?"

"No. I don't mean she's the murderer. I mean, she's the motive. Trent is the one who popped her."

"What?" said Trent incredulously. "Are you saying I popped her? Now look here, you. You can't go around making accusations like that about me or about Melissa either. She's a nice girl and I won't stand for anybody talking about her."

"I knew it! I knew it!" Humphrey chortled. "You're talking up for her and that means only one thing—you're crazy for her."

"I am?" said Trent. "For *her?*"

"Yup. This business about your wife hiring Doan to watch you is a gag. Your wife is completely in your power. She does exactly what you tell her and nothing else. She wouldn't dare hire a detective to watch you."

"This one is going to be really something extra," Doan observed. "Keep on, Humphrey."

"Your wife may be paying Doan," Humphrey said to Trent, "but it's you who tells him what to do, and what you told him to do this time was to watch Melissa Gregory."

"Why?" Trent asked blankly.

"I told you. You're crazy for her, and you suspected she was falling for this Frank Ames. There wasn't any masked prowler last night. You have a key to her apartment, and you were waiting for her when she came home. You popped her one for going out with Ames."

"I did this?" Trent asked, stunned.

"Yes, you. She squawked before you popped her, and this Beulah Porter Cowys came blundering in and saw and heard enough to know what really happened. You called the cops in an attempt to cover things up with that nut-wagon story about a guy with his head in a silk stocking. You didn't fool Beulah Porter Cowys any. She went over to Hollywood this afternoon to shake your wife down by telling your wife about you and Melissa Gregory. She wouldn't have gotten any change out of your wife, like I said, but you had to knock her off anyway because Doan had knocked off Ames, and Beulah Porter Cowys might have sounded off about that."

"I wondered when I was going to appear in this," Doan observed.

"You'd been following Ames and Melissa," Humphrey told him. "You were out in front of the building, lurking around like you usually are. Ames saw or heard something, and he got out of his car, intending to go on up and take this Trent all apart for batting Melissa Gregory around. That damned dog of yours took out after Ames and ran him into the alley and cornered him, and you cut Ames' throat."

"Who shot at me?"

"Nobody. You had two guns. You fired one off in the air and then gave it to that damned Carstairs, and he buried it in one of those vacant lots around there."

"I congratulate you, Humphrey," said Doan.

"This is incredible!" Trent choked. "This is the most absolutely fantastic tissue of criminal nonsense that I've ever listened to!"

"That's all right, bub," said Humphrey, nodding at him meaningfully. "I just wanted you to know I'm on to you. And I always get my man."

"Crime doesn't pay," Doan added.

Something slid through the air between Trent and Doan with an ugly, slicing hiss. It hit the sidewalk right at Trent's feet and shattered into shrapnel-like splinters. It was a heavy, grooved roof tile.

"Gug?" said Humphrey, staring up.

"Just remember," said Doan, also looking up. "That Trent didn't throw that tile, and neither did I."

"Ah," said Humphrey. "Nobody threw—"

Somebody yelled, though. It sounded thin and high and far away. Glass tinkled faintly.

"My instruments!" Trent gasped. He lunged up the steps.

"Wait a minute, you!" Humphrey shouted. He tore into the hall and up the stairs after Trent, flipping up his coattails and fumbling for the revolver in his hip pocket.

Doan spun on his heel and ran back along the side of the building. He had his revolver out. The turf was soft and spongy and silent under his heels He shoved heedlessly through a hedge and faced the narrow, shadowed rear door of the building.

He waited, puffing a little. Nothing happened. Nothing came out. And then a snarling, half-muffled uproar drifted down to him. Humphrey's yapping voice rode on the crest of it.

Doan darted inside the building. He found the narrowly twisting back stairs and went up them four at a time. He whirled around a corner at the top and out into the main upper corridor and ran down it toward Melissa's old office. He stopped short in the doorway.

The office was well on its way to being torn to pieces. Morales and Professor Sley-Mynick occupied the vortex of a sort of a whirlpool in the middle of it, caroming first one way and then the other and screeching like men possessed. Professor Sley-Mynick had a constrictor-like grip around Morales' waist. Morales was pounding him on the top of the head with both fists and trying to kick him at the same time. Trent and Humphrey ran around and around the two of them, trying to get a grip somewhere.

Doan fired his revolver at the ceiling, and for the space of a heartbeat the furious action froze dead still.

Then Humphrey got Morales by the neck. "What do you think you're doing? What goes on—" He shook Morales like a rag.

Trent was trying to disengage Professor Sley-Mynick. The blubbery man's glasses were gone—trampled underfoot—and his fat face was twisted hideously, lumpy mustache twitching and writhing like a live thing.

"What is it?" Trent demanded. "What happened?"

Professor Sley-Mynick collapsed into a half-sitting position. *"Geheim Staatspolizei!"* he cried, pointing a wavering finger at Morales. *"Geheim Staatspolizei! Yah, Yah!"*

"Christian pig!" Morales spat at him.

Humphrey shook him again. "Shut up! What's the old guy saying?"

"Geheim Staatspolizei is German," Trent said, puzzled. "It means German State Security Police, I think."

"Sure," said Doan. "The Gestapo."

"Gestapo?" Humphrey repeated. "Them guys is all in jail or hung or something."

"Nein!" Professor Sley-Mynick screamed. "No! He is! Him! That one!"

"Offspring of a she dog," said Morales.

Humphrey gave him another shake. "Keep your trap shut, or you're going to be missing some teeth. Trent, ask the fat guy what's going on."

Professor Sley-Mynick swallowed, groping furiously for

words. "Always they do it! Yes! *Geheim Staatspolizei!* They break things—smash them! Scientific things! They did mine in Hungary! Now he does it! This one! He smashes them on the roof! Yes, yes! Believe me! I saw him! On the roof!"

"My instruments!" Trent blurted.

The stepladder was still propped up in the corner under the square trap door in the ceiling. Trent swarmed up it and squirmed through and out of sight. Instantly his face reappeared, red and congested, peering down at them.

"My barometer and my anemometer are smashed, and there is something in my precipitation calibrator that certainly isn't dew!"

"Yes, yes!" said Professor Sley-Mynick, "I told you! Always they do it—*Geheim Staatspolizei!* Always they smash and break scientific instruments!"

Trent slid down the ladder. He advanced on Morales with his eyes narrowed dangerously and his upper lip lifted at one corner.

Humphrey jerked Morales back. "Get away from him," he warned Trent, "or I'll slap you one with this pistol. I'm running this bazaar. This crum bum doesn't look like any Gestapo to me. Did you smash those instruments and shy a tile at Trent, dope?"

"Yes," said Morales.

Humphrey stared at him, taken aback. "You did? Well, what the hell for?"

"He is a blasphemer."

"Huh?" said Humphrey.

"What?" said Trent. "What am I?"

"A pig," said Morales. "A blasphemous, illegitimate Christian pig."

"Well, why?" said Trent. "What did I do?"

"Your existence and your pretensions are an impious mockery. By your very presence you deny the existence of Quezatepequez."

"Who" said Humphrey groggily. "What?"

"Quezatepequez," said Trent. "That sounds like an Aztec word."

"Mayan, illiterate fool!" Morales snapped. "Quezatepequez is the great and only lord of Tegueigalpa— lord of the dark sky and the thunder bird. And you—you!—attempt to read his mind and predict his moods! I can do that—only I—a hereditary priest of the clan of Tegueigalpa!"

"Where does Maximilian come into this'?" Doan inquired.

"Faugh! I spit on his name! I use it only to mock Christian pigs!"

"This guy is a nut," Humphrey stated. "I can see that without going any further. He should be locked up, and that's just what's going to happen to him. Come on now, screwloose, or you'll think the thunder bird laid an egg right on your noggin."

"I'm coming along, too," said Doan. "Take care of Sley-Mynick, Trent. I'll holler up some help for you below-decks."

"What was all that the old guy was yipping about the Gestapo?" Humphrey asked.

"They pinched him once," Doan explained. "They evidently wrecked his laboratory as well as him when they did it. When he saw Morales working out on Trent's instruments, he made a connection."

"There are too many nuts around here," Humphrey said darkly, "and them that ain't are worse. What do you want to come along with me for?"

"You're going to succeed in arresting me sooner or later. I want to see what kind of service I can expect. Besides, this guy strikes me as sort of violent. Maybe you'll need some help."

"And I suppose you'd give me some if I did?"

"You'd be surprised."

"Oh, no, I wouldn't," said Humphrey.

CHAPTER FIVE

IT IS WELL RECOGNIZED BY THE authorities responsible for law enforcement that students very seldom commit any very serious crimes, with the exception of attending college, and that a jail is not quite in tune with the reverent inattention to worldly matters current on a campus. Consequently the sheriff's office, university substation, was tucked away unobtrusively on a residential street north of the campus and camouflaged under a green tile roof and behind spotless off-white walls. Even the steel bars on the windows were fluted and painted black to imitate ornamental iron grilles. But then, in Hollywood they have a habit of disguising the functional purposes of many buildings, both public and private, as witness a movie house that looks like a Chinese temple, a movie star's home built in the style of a Venetian bordello, gas stations designed on the igloo principle and a funeral parlor, the facade of which might be mistaken for the entrance to a race track or an amusement park.

Humphrey dragged Morales, who was very much on his dignity now, up the neat, narrow walk and in through the polished oak doors. Doan trailed negligently along behind them.

The receiving room of the substation was as clean and barren and impersonal as a military adjutant's office in a staging area. There were some chairs and a bench and a uniformed deputy sitting behind a long, low desk with four telephones, a ledger, and an interoffice communicator on it. The deputy had the air of a man who wouldn't know quite what to do about it if something did.

Morales advanced to the middle of the room and stopped short and looked around to make sure he had everyone's undivided attention. "Now," he said impressively.

He reached inside his shirt and brought out an oblong packet of yellow oiled silk. The silk rustled slickly as he unfolded it. He handed the papers inside to Humphrey.

"What?" said Humphrey.

Doan looked over his shoulder. The top sheet contained a photograph of Morales, some fingerprints, and a very impressive gold and ebony seal.

"This is in Spanish," said Humphrey.

"Can you read it?" Morales asked.

"No."

Morales snorted. "Is there no one in this pigsty who has any culture?"

Humphrey glared at him and then nodded to the desk deputy. "Call Hernandez."

The deputy flipped the switch on the communicator. "Hernandez! Front and center!"

One of the doors at the rear of the room opened, and a thin, gray-haired man came in and peered at them through thick horn-rimmed glasses.

"Read these, "Humphrey ordered, handing him the papers. "They belong to this bird."

Hernandez scanned the top sheet. "Well!" he said suddenly. He looked curiously at Morales. "He's a captain—that's a heavy rank—in the Coahuila State Police."

"What?" Humphrey said incredulously. "What police?"

"Coahuila. It's a state in Mexico. Right below the border." Hernandez was reading the next sheet. "Hey! Here's a letter from the Mexican ambassador to the United States asking that the guy be extended all aid and courtesy. And here's another saying the same thing from the American ambassador to Mexico. And here's one from the State Department—and one from the Mexican Department of State! And whoops! Here's one from the FBI. You'd better drop this guy quick—before he burns your fingers clear off!"

"Are those about a bird named Morales?" Humphrey inquired, still incredulous.

Hernandez flipped back to the top sheet. "Nope. The guy's name is Sebastian Rodriguez y Ruiz. But Sebastian Rodriguez y Ruiz has this guy's face and this guy's description."

"I am Sebastian Rodriguez y Ruiz," said Morales. "Morales is merely an alias I adopted. Are you satisfied now as to my real identity? If you like, you may call the Mexican Consul for Los Angeles. He knows me."

Humphrey stared at him, goggle-eyed. "Well, what's the big idea? I mean, going around acting like a janitor and a thunder bird and whatever?"

"May we have a little more privacy?"

"Sure. Come along."

Humphrey led the way through another door at the back of the room and along a short hall into a smaller office.

"Take that chair," he said. "Now what . . .Wait a minute." He pointed his finger at Doan. "We can't use you. Scram."

"No," said Sebastian Rodriguez y Ruiz. "I want him to hear what I say. I have my reasons."

"Oh, all right. Get going."

"I am concerned with a matter of very great importance. I repeat that so you will understand it clearly—*of very great importance.*"

"I get you," said Humphrey.

"In the State of Coahuila there is a very ancient, very revered religious shrine. I will not identify it further for reasons that will become clear as I proceed. The shrine was built and blessed in the sixteenth century. In it there were a number of sacred parchment scrolls."

"Yeah," said Humphrey eagerly.

"These scrolls are enormously valuable for a number of reasons. Historically, because of their contents. Commercially, because they were ornamented in gold leaf by several of the greatest artists then living. Religiously, because they are believed to have miraculous powers by the people who worship at the shrine."

"Yeah," said Humphrey. "Yeah."

"The scrolls were stolen."

"Ah-ha!" Humphrey exclaimed.

"They must be recovered. I repeat—they must be recovered."

"You bet," said Humphrey. "Positively. I can see that. Who hooked them?"

"Horace Trent."

"Yah-ha!" Humphrey chortled, "I knew all the time—What? *Horace Trent?*"

"Yes. Eric Trent's brother."

"Well, well, well," said Humphrey.

"Horace Trent," Sebastian Rodriguez y Ruiz said, "Claims to be an archeologist. He specializes in the theft of ancient objects of art of one sort or another. If he can't steal them, he fakes them. Eric Trent sells them for him."

"I knew it," said Humphrey. "I knew it all the time."

"Horace Trent," Sebastian Rodriguez y Ruiz went on, "is in jail now in Mexico. But he sent those scrolls—disguised as weather maps—to Eric Trent before I could find him and arrest him. Again, I must emphasize that it is of much more vital importance to get those scrolls than it is to arrest these two criminals. Eric Trent is perfectly capable of destroying them to clear himself—and, incidentally, his brother. That is why I assumed the identity of Morales, the idiot janitor. I wished to watch Eric Trent without him having any suspicion of me."

"Why did you bust his instruments?"

"That fool of a professor caught me searching Trent's office, so I broke the instruments to take his mind off the search. It did. Then I had to explain breaking the instruments by that nonsense about thunder birds, so Eric Trent wouldn't get suspicions of my actions. Eric Trent is very clever and very dangerous."

"And how," Humphrey agreed. "But, say? You shouldn't have said all this in front of Doan. He's probably in on that scroll deal. If he isn't, he'll try to steal them himself from Trent. I'd better lock him up right now."

"No. He is the one who is going to get those scrolls for me."

"He is?" Humphrey asked.

"Yes. He is in Trent's confidence. He can find out where Trent has hidden them—that is, if he doesn't already know."

"Man alive!" Humphrey protested. "You can't trust Doan. He's no straighter than a snake."

Sebastian Rodriguez y Ruiz smiled in a very sinister way. "This time he will be honest. Because if he does not get me those scrolls I will testify that I saw him kill Frank Ames."

"What!" Humphrey yelled, coming half out of his chair. "You saw—Doan, I hereby arrest you for murder!"

Sebastian Rodriguez y Ruiz sighed wearily. "Please restrain

yourself. I am not going to testify that he killed Frank Ames if he returns the scrolls."

"You're not—" said Humphrey groggily, floundering around two laps behind. "You're not going to—"

"No! Must I keep repeating and reiterating that the recovery of those scrolls is of absolutely paramount importance? The murder is a minor matter."

"But—but you saw Doan—"

"Certainly. I was the prowler."

"Ugh," said Humphrey, completely lost now.

"Kindly pay attention to what I am saying. I was searching for the scrolls at the time Melissa Gregory surprised me. I thought Trent might have persuaded her to hide them for him."

"But you saw Doan—"

"Yes!"

"Oh, boy," said Humphrey, blowing out a long, gusty sigh of relief. "At last. I've got him. You'll have to testify against him whether you want to or not."

"I think you are a complete fool," said Sebastian Rodriguez y Ruiz. "You had better refer again to that letter from the Mexican Department of State. I have diplomatic immunity."

Humphrey stood up and threw his chair into the corner. He raised his fists and shook them impotently at the ceiling.

"Why does everybody I pinch have to have friends or immunity or drag or influence or some damned thing? Why? Why? What have I done to deserve this?"

When no one answered him, Humphrey lowered his fists to his sides and for a moment he looked beaten. But then a crafty light came into his eyes and he regarded Sebastian Rodriguez y Ruiz intently.

"There's one thing your diplomatic immunity doesn't protect you against," he said. "If I accuse you of murder—unless you testify against Doan—there's nothing you can do about it."

Sebastian Rodriguez y Ruiz gave a loud and long Latin laugh. He hooked out an arm pointed a finger at himself. "Me of murder? *Me?* Tell me, please, who have I murdered?"

"Frank Ames," Humphrey said. "As a matter of fact I could whip up a pretty good case against you. Already you've confessed being the prowler. That puts you on the scene. All I really need to prove now is intent and motive."

Sebastian Rodriguez y Ruiz started laughing again. When he had finished, he spat out one word: "Ridiculous!" And then, drawing himself up, crossing his arms on his chest and patting one foot impatiently, he said, "And what about Beulah Porter Cowys? I suppose I am supposed to have killed her too? Maybe I disguised myself as a sunlamp or a permanent waving machine and sneaked into Heloise of Hollywood's Beauty Salon?"

"Maybe," said Humphrey.

"And maybe not," said Sebastian Rodriguez y Ruiz with a positive air. "Do you happen to know a most attractive young graduate student at the university named Shirley Parker? Well, whether you do or not makes no difference. Miss Parker is a special. She is taking her master's in psychology. She is writing a thesis on sexual behavior—at least sexual behavior has something to do with it—and I am trying to help her by providing her with material . . .Well, it so happens that at the precise time and moment when Beulah Porter Cowys was killed, I was embarked on a little matter of research for my friend Miss Parker. I was, in fact, in the company of a most attractive young blonde who, though for the moment shall be nameless, could be induced I am sure, in view of the pleasure she seemed to derive out of the assistance she gave me in the research, to testify at the proper time that . . ."

"What?" Humphrey interrupted. "Get to the point."

"I have an alibi," Sebastian Rodriguez y Ruiz told him. "An iron clad alibi, as you stupid Americans say. Accuse me of killing anybody or anything and I'll sue you for libel, slander, false arrest, both malfeasance and misfeasance in office, but mostly for malicious prosecution. Accuse me of something—just you dare! I'll sue you for one hundred thousand dollars or maybe one million dollars!"

"Rot!" Humphrey came back at him. "Nonsense! If you refuse

to testify against Doan, I'll arrest you just as fast as that . . ." And he snapped his fingers. "In fact," he shouted, now completely beside himself with rage and frustration, "I'll arrest anybody I want to for anything I want to so long as I—as I wear this badge." He pointed to the shield on his vest.

With an unobtrusive but nevertheless lightning quick motion, the Mexican reached over, jerked off the shield and threw it to the floor.

"Your outbursts are distasteful to me," Sebastian Rodriguez y Ruiz informed Humphrey. "I shall leave now, but I advise you to remember everything I told you and to act accordingly. I do not propose to be thwarted by your stupidity. Come with me, you."

Doan followed him meekly along the hall and out through the receiving room.

Sebastian Rodriguez y Ruiz stopped on the steps and nodded coldly. "I shall expect you to search out those scrolls and turn them in to me at once."

"You just go right ahead and expect," Doan invited.

"Aren't you going to do it?"

"No."

"Did you hear what I just told Humphrey?"

"Yes."

"Well?"

"That was a very interesting story," said Doan. "Of course, there was one little discrepancy in it. Eric Trent doesn't have a brother named Horace. In fact, Eric Trent doesn't have any brothers at all. Good-by for now, Sebastian. I'll be seeing you."

It was nine o'clock when Doan came in the front door of the Pericles Pavilion. He had just spent a couple of hours talking long distance to Mexico City. This is a hazardous occupation which, besides time and money, requires persistence, patience, a loud voice, an extensive vocabulary, and a strong constitution. Right now, Doan was dragging his heels.

The door of the Aldriches' apartment opened, and the duplicate Aldrich faces, superimposed one above the other like carbon copies, peered disapprovingly out at him.

"Good evening," said Doan.

The Aldriches continued to peer—in silence.

Doan tried again. "Good evening."

The Aldriches said: "We do not approve of murder. We do not feel that we can longer acknowledge your acquaintance." Their door closed. Immediately it opened again. "Or that of your dog," said the Aldriches. The door closed.

Doan shook his head and went on up the stairs. He knocked on the door of Melissa's apartment. There was no answer. He went on up to the third floor and tried Trent's apartment. The door was unlocked, and he opened it.

Carstairs was lying on the chesterfield with his head dangling over one end and his tail over the other. He was snoring.

Doan went in and looked around. There was a note fastened to the lamp shade with a bobby pin. Doan read it. It was from Melissa, and it said:

> *I am going to the Get Acquainted Dance at Dullwich Hall with Eric Trent. I persuaded Carstairs that I didn't need a bodyguard just for that, because after all, Eric isn't the murderer, is he?*

Under this, in different handwriting, was the one word: No.

Doan studied that "No" uneasily. He was wondering just who wrote it. After a moment, he put the note down and took the large volume with the Greek title from Trent's bookcase. He opened it with an air of wistful anticipation. It was empty.

"Oh, hell," said Doan.

The telephone rang.

Doan picked it up. "Yes?"

"Is Eric Trent there?"

"No. This is Doan."

"This is Heloise of Hollywood. Where is Eric, Doan?"

"I don't know."

"Well, suppose you find out."

"Okay," said Doan.

"And when you do—tell him I want to see him. I mean, tonight."

"Okay."

"Up at my house. Tell him he can bring that Melissa Gregory mess along. I know he's with her."

"Okay."

"And after that—you're all through."

"What?" said Doan.

"I won't be needing you any more. I'll pay you up to the end of next week if you don't hike your expense account too high."

"Before I exit smiling, I should maybe give you an item or two of information I uncovered."

"I have all the information I need. Just turn in your bill."

"Okay," said Doan.

"Go find Eric now. Don't stop to get drunk on the way."

"What do you mean—drunk?"

"You probably know the meaning of the word better than anybody I ever came across, Doan. I mean soused and stinko and looping and polluted like I've seen you more times than I can count on both the toes and fingers of all my customers."

"You're maligning me," said Doan. "My mother wouldn't like to hear you talk about me like that—that is, if she could hear."

"Get going."

"Okay."

Doan hung up, and then he reached down and put his thumb across Carstairs' nostrils. Carstairs reared up on the chesterfield, snorting like a grampus.

"I'm not me, really," Doan told him. "You're having a nightmare and I'm a part of your bad dream."

Carstairs looked at him incredulously, raising his eyebrows.

"You're still asleep," Doan said. "The only reason you aren't resting peacefully is that you ate something that disagreed with you."

Carstairs yawned, settled back down on the chesterfield again and closed his eyes.

"Dope!" Doan shouted, and Carstairs jumped up alertly. "Dope, dope, dope, dope, dope. You'd believe anything anybody told you . . . Come on, we've got business."

Somewhere or other T. Ballard Bestwyck had picked up the idea that the student serfs under his sovereign sway would like to know each other at least slightly. This naive notion was treated with the contempt it deserved by the normal members of the student body, but that didn't stop T. Ballard Bestwyck from throwing contests he called Get Acquainted Dances everywhere, anywhere and incessantly. No one ever attended them but the bedeviled members of the faculty who were drafted into supervising them and assorted coveys of drips and drools who, upon their arrival, chose up sides according to their sexes, threw out battle lines on opposite edges of the dancing arena, and spent the evening smirking and sneering at each other in frantic frustration.

Things were going normally when Doan and Carstairs arrived at Dullwich Hall, which was a dreary sort of a place, very appropriately named. Several of the faculty couples had ventured out into the no man's land between the battle lines out of sheer boredom and were pushing each other pointlessly around to a natty arrangement of *Japanese Sandman* played by two feeble fiddles and a rheumatic piano.

Melissa and Eric Trent were among them. Melissa wasn't exactly beaming, but Trent was making very heavy weather of it. His blond hair was sweatily matted, and he was breathing through his mouth, and his eyes roamed ceaselessly in search of succor. He saw Doan and stopped short. Melissa half-tripped. Trent straightened her up and pointed at Doan. They came across the floor, avoiding the other rhythmic navigational hazards.

"Mr. Doan," said Melissa, "do you want me to be frank with you?"

"Sure," said Doan.

Melissa pointed. "He can't dance worth a damn."

"I told you I couldn't," Trent said. "Who do you think I could have practiced with the last few years—polar bears? You're the one who insisted that I try."

"I thought you were a man," Melissa said. "I thought you could stand on your own feet."

"I didn't step on you."

"Just because I'm exceptionally agile, you didn't."

"I can't dance."

"Well, all right," said Melissa. "I'm agreeing with you. That's what I just got through telling Doan. Why are you arguing with me?"

"I'm not."

"You are. And if you don't stop, I'm going to call you something I told you I wouldn't call you."

"And if you do, I'll do what I told you I'd do if you did."

"Do you think he would?" Melissa asked Doan.

"Yes," said Doan. "If you're thinking of calling him what I think you are. Whenever he hears that name, his strength becomes as the strength of ten."

"All right, then," said Melissa. "I won't call you that, but you can't stop me from thinking it at you."

"Oh, yes, I can," said Trent.

"Let's postpone this matter," Doan suggested, "before we get too metaphysical. I have a message for you both from Mrs. Heloise of Hollywood Tremaine Trent."

"Is it printable?" Melissa asked.

"Oh, yes. She wants to see you both up at her house—right away or anyway, pretty quick."

"We're not going," said Trent.

"Yes, we are," said Melissa. "I've got a few conversational tidbits I've dreamed up to try out on her. She got the jump on me last time. I can't think well when my feet are dirty. And, anyway, I want to see her house. I'll bet it's something, isn't it?"

"I don't know," said Trent. "I've never seen it."

Melissa stared at him. "What?"

"I started getting mad at Nome, Alaska, where I ran across

the first newsstand I'd seen in four years. By, the time I got to Seattle, I was steaming, and I boiled clear over before I arrived in Hollywood. We did our sparring in her lawyer's office."

Melissa patted him on the shoulder. "You're a good boy."

"Thank you. Doan, what happened to Morales? Melissa says those names he used were just nonsense words. No such clans or gods or whatnot exist."

"That's only the half of it," Doan informed him.

"Morales doesn't exist, either."

"What?"

"His real name is Sebastian Rodriguez y Ruiz, and he's a detective from Mexico."

"Well, why did he smash my instruments?"

"This one will stop you," said Doan. "He smashed them because your brother, Horace, stole some scrolls from a church in Mexico."

Trent just stared at him.

Doan nodded. "That's what he told Humphrey and Humphrey believed him."

"But why?"

"Because this Sebastian Rodriguez y Ruiz is a genius. I suspected that, and so I called up Mexico City, and they confirmed it. He is a positive, certified genius at detecting things. If you don't believe it, ask him."

"Another detective," Melissa groaned. "They're getting as thick around here as fleas on a chihuahua. When I started teaching here I thought this was a general arts university, but now it looks as though it's turning out to be a school for rookie cops. If I don't watch myself I'll wake up one day in a police matron's uniform with my name changed to Maggie O'Flaherty."

Trent turned to Doan. "But about this Morales, or Sebastian Rodriguez y Ruiz or whatever he calls himself. Why was he pretending to be a janitor?"

"I told you," said Doan. "He's a genius and genius is inscrutable."

Melissa tugged at Trent's arm. "Come on. I want to go see Heloise."

"Good-by, forever," said Doan.

"What?" said Melissa.

"Carstairs and I have now taken our humble place among the faceless army of the unemployed and unwelcome. We have been fired."

"Oh," said Melissa. "But we want to say good-by to you—I mean, in a big way. Wait here until we get back. You can dance with some of these girls."

Doan shivered. "Thank you," he said, "Thanks a million. But no thanks."

"Well, wait at Eric's apartment, then."

"It's a deal," said Doan. "That is, it's a deal at the moment. But I'm feeling sort of restless and I have a lot on my mind and I don't know where I may end up eventually."

The road up the canyon wasn't particularly steep, but its designers had done the best they could to make it appear so. It switched back and forth and doubled on itself like a snake with a stomach ache. The headlights of Trent's car illuminated it only about one tenth of the time; during the other nine tenths they swept pretty but aimless swaths in the night off to the right or left. The engine grumbled and complained to itself in a deeply outraged way.

"For goodness' sakes," said Melissa. "Shift into second before you pull a bearing."

"I might have known it," said Trent.

"Known what?"

"That you'd be one of these females who aren't satisfied with just backseat driving. In addition, you've got to run in a lot of senseless lingo you, picked up hanging around garages. Pull a bearing!"

"Well, people do!"

"Not people named Trent."

Melissa looked miffed. "I'm not as bad a backseat driver," she said, "as you are a dancer."

"I told you I don't like to dance," Trent informed her. "Also I'm out of practice." He took his eyes off the tortuous road for a moment and gave her a little smile. "But let's stop quarreling. As far as not liking dancing is concerned, I have this to say. I almost enjoyed dancing with you. If there hadn't been anyone else there, and even if there hadn't been any music and we'd been just standing there, I think I really would have enjoyed it"

Melissa turned to him but her lashes covered her eyes. "I wonder why?"

"Yes," Trent said, "I wonder." The smile disappeared from his face and for a moment he looked painfully serious. "I don't suppose it had anything to do with the fact that you were very close to me and I had my arms around you and all of a sudden I had the feeling . . ."

"Does Heloise of Hollywood make you feel that way too?" Melissa interrupted impishly.

"Oh, stop it!" Trent said. "Can't a guy get even a little bit sentimental with you without—well, just without?"

Melissa had to turn her head. Her shoulders were shaking with chuckles. "I suppose you'd get even more sentimental if I called you Han— Oooh! Don't you dare choke me! Look out! Grab the wheel! What are you trying to do—kill us both?"

A cliff jumped out at them and then jumped back in place when Trent, whose hands had been off the steering wheel and around Melissa's throat, grabbed the wheel again and gave the car a twist back into the road.

The headlights swished around like a scythe, and the tires squealed on a cutback curve.

"Go slower!" Melissa cried. "We're going to pass Heloise's place without seeing it."

"I can't go slower," Trent said, "without backing up."

"Wait, wait, wait!" Melissa shrilled. "I think that must be it! Clear back up there. Look for the gates, now."

"That's what I am doing."

"You missed them!"

"I did not."

"Oh, why do you have to be so stubborn and stupid? You must have missed them. You just weren't looking. Well, you'll just have to turn around—"

Two fat, high white-brick pillars swam smoothly at them out of the night.

"Yes?" said Trent gently. "Yes?"

"Oh, shut up."

Trent turned off on smoothly oiled macadam. The road dipped down, and then went up in a rush. Trent shifted into second, and they ground dismally upward.

"Gee," said Melissa. "Look."

They were up on the top of the butte now, and the house was waiting right there, poised and ready to pounce. It was enormous, squared off solid and dark against the sky, throwing a sullen shadow in deference to the moon. Trellised vines crawled sinuously black over the side walls, and the few lighted windows were like sly, peeping eyes.

"There's one thing I'm missing," Melissa observed, "and it bothers me. I wonder where Boris Karloff is?"

The road circled and widened at the front of the house. There was no veranda or porch. There were six wide stone steps leading up to an immense arched doorway sunk deep in the smooth stone. There were lights behind the thick-walled porthole windows on either side.

Trent stopped the car, and he and Melissa got out. The wind was soft and cool in their faces, and the moon seemed very far away. Their heels clicked lightly on the macadam and scraped a little on the stone steps.

"What do we do now?" Melissa asked." Yell 'Ahoy, the castle' or blow ourselves a fanfare?"

"This seems to be a bell," said Trent.

Chimes played a lingering, low melody somewhere inside. The house brooded and waited in utter silence.

"Well," said Trent, after a while, helplessly.

"Well, hell," said Melissa. She raised her fist and smacked the door one.

It swung back noiselessly.

"Glug," said Melissa. "Aren't we just having more darned fun, though?"

They were looking the length of a hall. It was a story and a half high, and the walls and ceiling were painted a dead white. The floor was black polished oak and there were white rugs spread along it like grotesque giant footprints.

"Homey," Melissa commented. "Let's go in."

They started along the hall, and their footsteps started following behind them in tapping echoes. Melissa took hold of Trent's arm.

There was a door to their right, and a door to their left. Both were closed. Trent and Melissa went reluctantly past them, and then Melissa said, "Wait. There's a light behind that one."

She rapped on it. The silence seemed to stir itself slightly, but there was no real sound. Melissa tried the long, wrought-iron latch on the door. It clicked, and the door moved back, softly reluctant.

The room was a library. The walls from ceiling to floor were lined with shelves of books. The books looked like they had been taken out often—and dusted and put right back again. Facing the door, at the end of the room, there was a desk that was a solid block of black wood as big as a dining room table.

Heloise of Hollywood was sitting behind the desk. She was wearing a blue tailored dress, and her hair was meticulously unswept. Her head was tilted a little to one side, and she was staring at them with an air of polite, dead interest.

"Oh," Melissa murmured. "Oh."

Trent whispered to himself.

Very slowly they advanced, holding hands like reluctant children. One of Heloise's hands—the nails were a polished, appropriate purple—was lying on the desk top with the lax fingers just touching a fat, ugly automatic with a snub nose. Trent and Melissa were closer now, and they could see the very small, neatly dark hole in her left breast. Blood had darkened the cloth of her dress below it, but it was hardly noticeable.

"She shot herself," said Melissa. Her voice croaked ridiculously on the words, and she swallowed hard.

"No, she didn't," said Trent. "There's no powder burn on her dress. And that's an 8 millimeter Mauser on the desk. It would make a much bigger hole."

"Would—would a .22 make a hole like—like . . ."

"Yes."

"Oh, my," said Melissa. "Doan said my prowler had a .22."

"Well, there's one thing," said Trent slowly, "Humphrey can't claim Doan did this. He's not here."

"But you are," said Melissa. "And, what's more, so am I."

The telephone rang. It was on a circular stand at Heloise's left hand. Trent and Melissa waited with a sort of dread fascination for her to answer it. She didn't.

It rang again.

Melissa walked gingerly around the desk and picked it up. "Hello."

A voice like thick plush said: "Good evening This is T. Ballard Bestwyck. May I speak to Heloise?"

"Well," said Melissa, "no."

"I beg your pardon?"

"You can't speak to her. I mean, she can't speak to you, which amounts to the same thing, doesn't it?"

"I don't think you understood me, young woman. I am T. Ballard Bestwyck. I'm the president of—"

"I know. I work for you."

"What was that?"

"I teach at the university."

"What's your name?"

"Melissa Gregory."

"Well, it's about time?"

"What?" said Melissa blankly.

"I was just calling Heloise to apologize for your brazen behavior. Now that you're up there, you can do it yourself. And you'd better be very humble about it, young woman. There's a moral turpitude clause in your contract, and if you don't let other women's husbands alone you're going to find yourself involved in a serious situation."

The line suddenly crackled. T. Ballard Bestwyck hadn't hung up. There was no dial tone. The line was dead.

Melissa turned her head slowly to look at Trent.

"What's the matter?" Trent demanded.

"Somebody—cut the line."

The lights went out.

"Eric!" Melissa cried. "Oh, Eric—"

She grabbed him and clung to him desperately, both arms about his neck.

"I'm so sc-scared," she whimpered, "and you shouldn't mind. J-just a few minutes ago you s-said you liked to be close to m-me and have your arms about m-me . . ."

"My arms aren't about you," Trent said, obviously trying to remain calm. "Yours are about me, but it's all right, Melissa. Heloise won't mind now—not any more."

The half door boomed shut and the lock clicked coldly and Melissa gasped.

"All right," Trent said. "Start screaming. That's just what we need at this point."

"I've never screamed in my life!" Melissa retorted, and immediately afterward began screaming her head off. "Eeeh! Oow! Eeeh! Eep!"

Trent slapped at her. He missed her face in the darkness and hit her on the back of the head. Melissa stopped screaming.

Something scraped very gently in the hall, and then without warning there were three shots—very close together, sharp and bitingly distinct. Instantly there was another shot. This was a heavier, louder thud.

After that there was silence. It was not a pleasant or comforting silence. Melissa breathed against Trent's coat collar with her mouth open.

Something tapped lightly on the hall door.

Doan's voice murmured, "Trent. Melissa."

"In here," said Trent. "The door is locked."

The lock clicked again and the shadows moved vaguely.

"Are you two all right?" Doan asked.

"I guess so," said Trent.

"Come closer to the door here. I want to watch the hall. I chased the guy back inside. He's holed up in the house somewhere now."

Trent and Melissa shuffled forward cautiously. They could see a vague, bent outline that was Doan. The barrel of his revolver gleamed a little in the dimness. He had the hall door almost shut and was watching through the narrow opening.

"He'll run out the back," Trent said.

"He'll maybe try. Carstairs is out there."

They waited tensely.

"Heloise is dead," Trent said in an undertone. "Over at her desk. She was shot."

"Yeah," said Doan. "I thought I'd better come up and warn her even if she didn't want me to. She thought she could handle the guy. She could just as well wrap up a tiger in a paper napkin."

"She had a gun."

"Sure. She had twenty servants, too."

"Where did they go?"

"They're locked up downstairs somewhere—probably in the wine cellar. I've got no time to go fishing around for them now. I've got a hunch I'm going to get myself killed as it is. This guy is hell on wheels with that pistol of his. He mistook a tree for me a minute ago, or I'd be past worrying at this point."

Carstairs let go with a bellowing halloo. The .22 cracked twice precisely. Carstairs bellowed angrily right back at it.

"He's under cover," Doan breathed "If he only has brains enough to stay that way."

The pistol cracked futilely again. Carstairs let his bellow out another notch, and the whole night began to throb with it.

"Stay in here," Doan ordered "I'm going a-hunting, and I'm going to shoot at anything that even looks like it might move. I'm scared green of this guy." He opened the door wider. "Stay right here. I mean it. Oh, why do I get myself into situations like this? I must be crazy."

He faded noiselessly into the darkness.

CHAPTER SIX

TRENT AND MELISSA WAITED TAUTLY. The silence pressed in on them as thick as black butter. One century crawled past. And then another.

Doan's revolver thudded. Trent jumped involuntarily, and Melissa whimpered against his coat.

The silence crept back and surrounded them. Doan's revolver thudded again. The .22 cracked back at it spitefully this time. Someone yelled, fiercely incoherent. Feet raced across bare flooring. Something fell over with a crash that made the air shudder. A door slammed dully.

"I can't take this," Trent said. "I've got to help him. You stay here."

"Oh, no! Oh, no!"

"Stay right close behind me, then. Walk in step with me."

They went out into the hall like a queer four-legged bug. Melissa was clutching the back of Trent's coat in both fists. She could feel the muscles in his back, rigid and tensed. They moved slowly, and the darkness moved right with them, unchanging.

"Steps," Trent whispered.

They went up them—a lot of them. And then there was a cold, slow click just over their heads.

Doan said: "Trent?"

"Yes."

"You're lucky," said Doan. "That's the time you didn't get killed. Come on up here."

They were in a hall.

"Did you hit him when you shot?" Trent asked.

"Hell, no. I did run him into the bedroom there, though. The one behind that door. And if he thinks I'm going in there after him, he's crazy."

Carstairs barked from somewhere outside on an inquiring note.

Doan cupped his hands and bellowed through them "Yes! I'm still with you! Stay out there! Watch!"

Carstairs barked again, momentarily pacified.

"Well, what are we going to do now?" Trent asked.

"Call the cops," Doan said, keeping his gun pointed at the bedroom door. "Let them root him out. They're expendable."

"The telephone line is cut. It was cut at the same time the lights were switched off. Melissa was talking on it."

"This guy," said Doan, "thinks of everything. Okay. We'll starve him out. How are we fixed for supplies? Have you got a drink on you?"

"No."

"All right. Go on down and unlock the servants. Send a bottle back up here by one of them. We'll fight it out on this line if it takes all summer."

Trent said uneasily: "Maybe he'll shoot through the door at us."

"Not that door. It's a two-inch hardwood slab. A .22 won't punch through it."

The .22 smacked from inside the bedroom. Carstairs yelled in furious indignation. The .22 smacked again instantly. Carstairs bellowed right back, but the tone of his voice was slightly muffled now.

Doan let his breath out. "He got under cover again. He's going to get his brains blown out if he doesn't stop playing around . . . Carstairs! Stay where you are! Down! Keep down!"

Carstairs barked once, defiantly. Then he cut loose in a continuous, urgent, racketing uproar.

"What now?" said Doan, listening tensely.

Wood creaked faintly.

"He's climbing out the window!" Down exclaimed.

He aimed his revolver at the lock on the door and fired and

then fired again. Wood splintered, and the smell of burned powder was sharp and acrid in the hall. Doan slammed his heel against the door above the lock, slammed it again below the lock. He shouldered into the door hard, hammering at the lock with the butt of his revolver.

Metal gave with a sudden rasp, and the door banged violently open. Doan fell flat on his stomach, half in and half out of the bedroom, revolver pushed ahead of him. He stayed that way, rigid, watching.

"What?" Trent whispered, crouched against the wall beside the doorway. "What?"

Doan spoke without turning his head. "I think he's on the trellis outside the window."

Moving vines made a leafy, ripping sound.

"Yeah!" said Doan, lunging to his feet. "Carstairs! Carstairs! Guard!"

Carstairs roared willingly from outside and below. The vines crackled.

"Now what will I do?" Doan demanded. "If I poke my head out that window, he'll pop it off for me. If I run outside, he'll come back in this way."

"Another bedroom. . ." Trent suggested.

The vines rattled and slithered more loudly.

"Back!" Doan ordered urgently. "He's coming back up! Get out of the doorway!"

Something crawled up eerily at the lower corner of the open window. Moonlight glinted on the long, pencil-like barrel of the .22 pistol. It groped around blindly and then suddenly spat. Flame streaked slantwise toward the ceiling.

"Ah," said Doan.

He was aiming carefully with his revolver, steadying his right wrist with his left hand. He fired. The .22 automatic spun up into the air, glistening sleekly, and then thudded loosely on the floor.

"I did it!" Doan chortled. "I've always wanted to, and I did it! I shot a gun out of a guy's hand! Come in off that vine, screwloose! And don't try any funny work! I'm as good as Red Ryder!"

Wood suddenly tore loose in a long drawn, ripping screech.

"What—" said Doan.

He raced across the bedroom to the window with Melissa and Trent stumbling along behind him. The moon was ghastly bright now, and in its light, suspended incredibly in space ten feet out from the window, was something large and black, black and crouched and malignant that screeched at them.

The lattice work was propping it up there, unbelievably, like a weirdly extended, clumsy stilt. Then the lattice swayed further and lost its last hold on the wall with a series of popping reports and began to fall, crumpling in on itself, away from the house.

The black figure mouthed incoherent, terrified sounds, twisting in the air. And directly under it, gleaming like quicksilver, was the slickly sullen surface of Heloise's swimming pool. The lattice hit the edge of the pool, and the water opened up with a resounding boom.

Carstairs raced his shadow across the lawn and skidded on the edge of the pool.

"Carstairs!" Doan shouted. "Stay out of there! Let him drown, and save the state money! Stay out—"

Carstairs dove into the pool.

"Oh, hell's fire!" Doan exclaimed angrily.

He whirled away from the window and ran out of the bedroom. Trent tore down the stairs after him, jerking Melissa along behind with a viselike grip on her wrist. They drummed along the hall and out the front door and around the side of the house.

Doan pulled out ahead of them going down the slope of the lawn. His heels grated on the tiled edge of the pool. The surface of the water was ripped and torn to froth, and then Carstairs' head heaved up out of it. He had a black, chunky, limp arm gripped in his jaws, and he was coughing in half-strangled snorts.

"Let go!" Doan yelled. "Let him drown! Who cares? Come here! Here! Here!"

Carstairs kept his grip and plowed away determinedly at the water. He came agonizingly closer. Doan leaned far out and grabbed the arm.

"All right! So you're a hero! Let go!"

Doan heaved back, and the black, ugly form slithered wetly out on the edge of the pool. Doan kicked it aside.

"Sit on him for a minute," he ordered no one in particular. "Carstairs! Now, come here, stupid! Here!"

Carstairs floundered against the side wall, and Doan got him by the collar. He hauled. Carstairs' forelegs flopped out on the tile. His back legs churned powerfully at the water. He came up and out suddenly, snorting and dripping.

Doan fell over backwards. "Now, watch out! Don't—Ow!"

Carstairs walked right over his prone form. He stepped aside, but not far enough aside, and shook himself.

"Floosh!" Doan sputtered. He sat up, wiping his face. "I'm going to kill you someday. I mean that seriously."

Carstairs stopped shaking and sat down and began to pant victoriously.

Melissa said in a small, stunned voice: "Mr. Doan, this— this—this is Professor Sley-Mynick."

"Yup," said Doan, getting to his feet. "Let's see if he's still working."

He knelt down beside the wet, black form. Professor Sley-Mynick's thin face was bluish and distorted, and little bubbles burst frothily on his lumpy mustache. Doan probed with exploring fingers.

"Cracked his skull," he stated. "Must have hit the bottom of the pool. He'll probably live, though."

"But—but did he . . ."

"He did," said Doan cheerfully. "He's your little old prowler in person."

"Oh!" Melissa exclaimed. "Then there was something awful and familiar . . . But what was he doing in my apartment?"

"It's just like I told you. He thought he was in Trent's apartment."

"What did he want in my apartment?" Trent demanded.

"I think he was going to fix up a nice little booby trap for you. That's why he had both the knife and the gun with him. He probably had a strip of rubber inner tubes and some nails with him, too. He was going to fasten the knife to the tube and the tube to the nails in such a way that when you opened the drawer, the tube would stretch and then flip the knife in your face. It's easy to fix up a trap like that if you know how."

"With a knife?" Trent said doubtfully. "That seems sort of uncertain."

"He didn't want to kill you. I mean, he didn't care whether he did or not. He just wanted to remove you from the campus. It didn't matter whether you were removed to the hospital or to the morgue."

"And Frank Ames?" Melissa said.

"There he was turning his car around when Sley-Mynick walked right out into the alley—and into Ames' headlights—busily engaged in peeling off that stocking mask. Ames recognized him at once. He stopped the car and got out to see what in the devil he was up to. You can see the fix that put Sley-Mynick in. There wasn't any story he could dream up that would pacify Ames permanently, because when Ames found out that the prowler had socked Melissa one, Ames was going to sound off like a fire siren. Sley-Mynick is not a man who takes long to make up his mind. He hadn't used his knife yet, and so now he did. He cut Ames' throat and dumped him in that garbage can, hoping to be able to drive in the alley and pick him up and tote him off somewhere and bury him. But he couldn't put that last idea over. Carstairs and I came snooping around after him. He shot at us and then he had to scram."

Melissa said, "And—and Beulah?"

"Remember what I said about how I went into her apartment and listened around? She couldn't have heard you yip if her door had been shut. I think she had her door open a little. I think she was snooping, just like the Aldriches were. I think she wanted to see whether or not Ames came up to your apartment with you."

Melissa nodded slowly. "Beulah was a little like that. She was nosey."

"And this time it was fatal. She saw the prowler. He ran past her door on the way out. I don't think she recognized him positively, or she would have said so. But she saw enough to make her wonder, because she was already wondering. Remember what she said when we were first talking about Sley-Mynick? She said he *was* a good biochemist—meaning he *had been.* Physics is sort of close to biochemistry, and Beulah Porter Coveys must have spotted something that Sley-Mynick did or said that made her a little leery. I mean, I suppose she was just sort of wondering about it vaguely, and this was something added. In any event, I'm sure she went around and talked to him the next morning, and he must have told her something that pacified her for the moment."

"What?" Trent demanded.

"I have no idea. He's a slicker. Anyway, Beulah Porter Cowys made a very bad mistake after that. She went to Heloise's place. That cooked her goose. I don't know whether she went there just to get her face fixed or whether she had some other reason. Neither did Sley-Mynick, I suppose. But he couldn't take a chance on her talking to Heloise about him. Carstairs' riot gave him his chance, although he would have managed it by some hook or crook anyway. That sort of wiped things up for Sley-Mynick. He'd had bad luck running into Ames and getting spotted by Beulah Porter Cowys, but now they were cleared away, and he went back after you again. He shied that tile at you. That probably wouldn't have killed you unless it hit you in the head, but it wouldn't have done you much good, either."

Trent said, "But *why—*"

Carstairs growled. Doan whipped around alertly, jerking the revolver from under his coat.

There was a man walking down the slope of the lawn toward them slowly and portentously, his shadow jigging eerily thin ahead of him.

"It's Morales!" Melissa gasped.

"Not any more," said Doan. "Now it's Sebastian Rodriguez y Ruiz, the great detective."

"How do you do," said Sebastian Rodriguez y Ruiz. "I see that, by sheer luck, you have managed to capture my quarry. You probably have no admissible evidence against him, so it is fortunate that I have arrived."

"What evidence have you?" Trent demanded.

"An unassailable case. I always make certain I have an unassailable case before I make an arrest. This man is demonstrably and unmistakably guilty of the murder of Herbert 'Big Tub' Tremaine in a cottage on the outskirts of Piedras Negras, State of Coahuila, Mexico, seven months and eleven days ago!'

"Who?" Trent said sharply.

"What?" said Melissa. "Big Tub Tremaine!" She stared accusingly at Doan. "You told me he had committed suicide!"

"I thought he had," said Doan. He looked at Sebastian Rodriguez y Ruiz. "Your authorities should file a little clearer reports."

"I suppose they do seem a little complicated to the dull-witted," Sebastian Rodriguez y Ruiz answered indifferently.

Doan said to Melissa: "The report said just what I told you— that Tremaine had heaved himself in the drink in front of a lot of witnesses, and that they'd had a lot of trouble fishing him out again. Well, the trouble was that it took them four days to recover his body, and by that time he was all chewed to pieces."

"But you said—he said—"

"I will explain the matter," said Sebastian Rodriguez y Ruiz, "because it involves some very brilliant feats of scientific detection. Big Tub Tremaine wished to flee to Mexico because he had embezzled some money from his wife. He had formerly worked in carnivals. He went down to Skid Row—a region in Los Angeles frequented by many vagrants—and located a character, a man he had known formerly in his carnival days, called Bumbershoot Bennie."

"Bumbershoot Bennie," Trent said numbly.

"Yes. Big Tub Tremaine hailed him with great joviality as a dear old pal. Big Tub Tremaine was going on a vacation trip to Mexico, he said, and nothing would do but that his old friend, Bumbershoot Bennie, should accompany him. But first he must buy Bumbershoot Bennie a new outfit of clothes. To show his great generosity and good heart, he would buy Bumbershoot Bennie an outfit as good as he was wearing himself. In fact, he would buy Bumbershoot Bennie an outfit exactly like the one he was wearing. He did."

"Oh," said Trent.

"Then," said Sebastian Rodriguez y Ruiz, "they started in Big Tub Tremaine's car for Ensenada. Somewhere along the road—as yet I don't know just where—Big Tub Tremaine killed Bumbershoot Bennie by beating him over the head with a tire iron. Then he tied a rope around Bumbershoot Bennie and threw him in the surf where there were some sharp rocks. He let Bumbershoot Bennie grind against the rocks for two days, until he was completely disfigured. Then he pulled the body in and put it in the rumble seat of his car."

"Oooh," said Melissa sickly.

"And then," said Sebastian Rodriguez y Ruiz, "he drove to Ensenada. He picked an appropriate spot and, secretly and by stealth, threw Bumbershoot Bennie in the ocean again. Next he put on a noisy performance in a bar, threatening loudly and dramatically to drown himself. Then he ran forth into the darkness, pursued by the people in the bar, and dove into the ocean. There was a wind, and the water was rough. It was at night, you remember. He swam under water away from the searchers, came ashore, and went his way. The police kept on searching until they found Bumbershoot Bennie's body, wearing Big Tub Tremaine's ring and his wrist watch, with Big Tub Tremaine's wallet in the pocket of a suit that obviously fitted the body and exactly matched the description of the clothes Big Tub Tremaine was wearing. It is quite understandable that in the circumstances they identified Bumbershoot Bennie's body as that of Big Tub Tremaine."

"And—and what next?" Melissa asked.

"Big Tub Tremaine wandered around, under various aliases, in Mexico for some two years. Finally he came to Piedras Negras, where he fell in with the murderous Sley-Mynick. And you can see what a temptation he offered to Sley-Mynick. He was already supposed to be dead, and in any event he was wanted as a criminal. He still had some of the money he had embezzled. Sley-Mynick murdered him and buried him in the patio of the cottage."

"Oh!" said Melissa. "But what in the world—"

"Pardon me. I am not finished yet. Sley-Mynick came to the university, thinking his murderous secret was safe forever, but he reckoned without Sebastian Rodriguez y Ruiz. I followed him relentlessly. And all would have been well if you had not appeared."

"Me?" said Trent.

"Yes. Naturally Sley-Mynick's evil conscience bothered him. He thought that Big Tub Tremaine's wife had gotten some inkling of his guilt and had set you to spy on him. He tried to get rid of you as he brushed aside the other fools who got in his way."

"Wait a minute," said Trent. "Why did you break my instruments?"

"I didn't. Sley-Mynick did that in an outburst of rage because he missed you with that tile he threw."

"Why didn't you say he did it—at the time?"

Sebastian Rodriguez y Ruiz said, "Sebastian Rodriguez y Ruiz has a reputation. I did not intend to have Sley-Mynick arrested until I was ready to do it myself."

"Sley-Mynick murdered Heloise. You caused her death by not speaking up about him when you should have."

Sebastian Rodriguez y Ruiz shrugged magnificently. "What of it? She is not Mexican. She was only an American."

"Well, so was Big Tub Tremaine."

"That is an entirely different matter. It must be known to all evildoers that they cannot murder anyone—not even an American—in the State of Coahuila without answering to Sebastian Rodriguez y Ruiz. Now I have wasted enough time here. You, Doan. Pick up the culprit and carry him to my car. I will go through the formalities and then return him to Mexico to meet his fate."

"He's wanted here for a few murders," Doan said.

"That is immaterial. I have a federal warrant certified and cleared by the state department. It takes precedence over local authority."

"Who is the warrant for?" Doan asked.

"For Sley-Mynick, naturally."

"Then it's no good, because this guy on the ground isn't Sley-Mynick."

"Are you insane?" Sebastian Rodriguez y Ruiz demanded.

"No. You did all right with your detection, but you didn't look hard enough at matters before you started. Just consider for a moment. On the one hand we have Big Tub Tremaine—a carnival tough guy, an embezzler and a murderer at least once. I think he'd done in several here and there before Bumbershoot Bennie, because you don't learn as much as he knew about murder just overnight. And on the other hand you have Professor Sley-Mynick—a poor beaten-up biochemist on the run from the Gestapo. Sley-Mynick and Big Tub Tremaine met in Piedras Negras, and one did the other in. Which one would be most likely to be the murderer?"

Sebastian Rodriguez y Ruiz said some things to himself in firecracker Spanish.

Doan smiled. "Sure. You slipped because Professor Sley-Mynick turned up and took his job as big as life."

"What are you talking about?" Trent demanded.

"Professor Sley-Mynick didn't kill Big Tub Tremaine. Big Tub Tremaine murdered Sley-Mynick. That's Big Tub Tremaine dying right there."

"Oh!" Melissa gasped. "Oh!"

"Don't you see what a wonderful deal this was for him?" Doan asked. "Big Tub Tremaine wanted to get back to the States. Probably he was fed up with Mexico and tortillas and enchiladas and frijoles and everything else Mexican—even the senoritas. That's the way with most fugitives. Before they commit their crimes they gloat over the dough they're going to grab and the life of luxury they're going to lead in some far away clime, but once they beat it out of the country they get homesick and the thing they want most in the world is to get back."

"I'm beginning to catch on," said Melissa.

"Of course," said Doan.

"Big Tub was afraid if he came back and the cops didn't spot him, his wife would—a fate worse than arrest."

"Exactly," said Doan.

"So he needed some place to hide," Melissa went on. "Also he needed some identity other than his own and a means of occupying himself respectably so that no one would suspect who he actually was."

"Smart girl," Doan told her. "Sley-Mynick's identity was ready-made for Big Tub. It included a job at a good salary and a nice refined, quiet place—the university—to hide as long as he wanted to. It was ideal. The fact that it was quite near, to where his wife had her beauty salon made little or no difference. When people are looking for something they're less likely to find it when it's stuck right under their nose."

"But Big Tub Tremaine wasn't a biochemist," Trent objected. "How could he hope to get away with such a disguise?"

"You forget," said Doan, "he was a onetime medicine show spieler. He could talk the lingo of drugs and chemicals and bell jars and test tubes right out of the pharmacopoeia. Whether or not what he said would make sense is something else again, but who were his undergraduate listeners to question whether the stuff their eminent European professor was giving them was straight from the shoulder fact or carnival doubletalk?"

Carstairs moved about restlessly, stopped in front of Doan, looked up and yawned.

"I know," Doan told him, "I bore you. But there are others present and they are interested, so keep still for a minute until I'm finished."

Carstairs lay down, crossed his paws and closed his eyes.

"Sure," said Doan, "for a long while Big Tub's disguise was perfect. He always had the Gestapo to fall back on, remember. Maybe he didn't know quite as much as he should about biochemistry. Well, his mind was confused and had been ever since he left Hungary. The Gestapo had knocked a good part of his knowledge out of him. And suppose he didn't look just exactly like the old Sley-Mynick. The Gestapo had disfigured him. And suppose he dodged people. The Gestapo had made him shy. Any possible slip he made, he could blame on the Gestapo, and no one would question him because his nerves were in such bad shape, poor man."

"I noticed he was pretty jumpy," Eric Trent said. He was standing talking to Doan but looking at and leaning close to Melissa and there was an expression on his face which seemed to indicate that he was thinking about something entirely different from what he was saying. "I noticed he was exceptionally jumpy every time that Shirley Parker was around. He avoided her like the plague."

"He had a reason there," Doan told him. "Shirley's a psychologist, isn't she? At any rate, a graduate student in psychology, and these psychologists and psychiatrists and the like have a way of seeing right through fakers and spotting a liar as soon as they talk to one. This guy was afraid of Shirley for that reason. It's a wonder he didn't murder her too, which would have been a shame, because aside from being a psychologist she's a remarkably pretty girl . . .Thinking the matter over and remembering the difficulty she was having getting together her material on sex, I wonder if I couldn't be of some help to her—maybe in a personal way. Do either of you happen to know her telephone number?"

"Never mind that now," Melissa said. "You tell us the rest—quick!"

"There isn't much rest. Everything was going along as smooth as silk for Big Tub—he knew nothing about Sebastian Rodriguez y Ruiz— alias Morales trailing him—and then Trent had to turn up. That blew things sky high. Big Tub knew who Trent was. He'd been keeping track of Heloise. He knew Trent was separated from her, but he knew very well that wasn't the end of the story. He knew Heloise didn't let go of things that were hers that easy. He knew she'd start hanging around the university, and if she did, sooner or later she was going to spot Big Tub. No disguise would fool her for an instant. If she spotted him, she'd have him in jail before he could wink, and that would mean getting it in the neck for Bumbershoot Bennie and Sley-Mynick on top of the embezzlement rap. He had to get Trent away from the university, and that was just what he was trying so hard to do."

"You told us about that," Melissa said. She, too, was talking to Doan, but she was looking at Trent who was still looking at her, and between them there seemed to be an intimacy born of a new discovery or a new thought. "That's what started the whole thing off. Sley-Mynick or Big Tub or whoever was fixing up a booby trap for Eric when I waltzed in and caught it in the noggin."

"That's right," said Doan.

"But Ames—and Beulah. . ."

"They got in his way. He was desperate. He had two murders—and probably more—behind him. He couldn't take any chances at all. He couldn't afford to have any attention directed toward him. He swatted them like the ordinary person would a couple of flies—Ames because Ames had seen him and Beulah Porter Cowys because she was nosing around and might say something to Heloise that would point Heloise at Big Tub, alias Sley-Mynick. He could easily prowl around in the beauty salon. He used to loaf there all the time. He knew the place like the palm of his hand, and Carstairs gave him a nice assist."

"I still want to know," Trent said, "why he smashed my instruments."

"You and your silly instruments," said Melissa, but there was no malice in her voice.

"They are not silly, and they are damned expensive."

Doan said, "He did that to cover himself after he missed with the tile and spotted Sebastian Rodriguez y Ruiz watching him. He was going to play his goofy blame-it-on-the-Gestapo game. Sebastian Rodriguez y Ruiz saved him the trouble by inventing that business about thunder birds."

"And another thing," said Trent. "What about my so-called brother, Horace?"

"Sebastian Rodriguez y Ruiz told Humphrey that because he thought Humphrey might possibly be bright enough to figure out that if Sebastian Rodriguez y Ruiz hadn't busted those instruments, only one other person could have. Sebastian Rodriguez y Ruiz did not intend to let Humphrey arrest the bird he thought was Sley-Mynick, so he pulled a herring in the shape of some nonexistent scrolls across the track."

"And you went off with the two of them and left me alone with Big Tub Tremaine—after he just got through trying to cave my head in with a tile! You're one hell of a bodyguard!"

"You were as safe as if you were in church," Doan assured him. "He wouldn't have dared make a move after that close shave. If he had killed you, even Humphrey would have known who did it."

"That would have been a big consolation," said Trent.

"Oh, Doan," said Melissa, "how awful. To think you could have been so heartless as to leave poor Eric alone and unarmed and unprotected in the company of this awful, awful person. I wouldn't have believed it of you. I've a good mind to strike your name off my list of nice people."

Doan looked at her blankly. "Your attitude," he said, "towards this guy—Eric. What's happened to change your attitude?"

"Never mind," said Melissa. "I want to know about Heloise."

"Sebastian Rodriguez y Ruiz went around to see her," Doan explained. He turned to the Mexican. "Didn't you do that?"

"Naturally," said Sebastian Rodriguez y Ruiz. He was looking very gloomy and very sullen and as though he had lost his last friend in the world somewhere far south of the Rio Grande.

Doan said, "Sebastian Rodriguez y Ruiz here wanted to know if there had been any previous connection—before Piedras

Negras, I mean—between Big Tub and Sley-Mynick. And while
he was at Heloise's, he showed her a picture of the fake Sley-
Mynick. So much is my assumption. Now let's see if I'm not
correct." Again he turned to the Mexican detective. "Isn't that
what happened?"

"Naturally."

"But Heloise fooled you. She didn't admit she knew him, did
she?"

"No."

"But she did," said Doan. "And how she did. She recognized
her dear departed husband's puss instantly. But Heloise never
did anything without figuring what effect it would have on the
business of Heloise of Hollywood. And this was something to
chew on—two murders and a dead husband turning up. But more
to the point, a husband she'd feel fine about never seeing again
inasmuch as she'd already proclaimed to the world her marriage
to Eric and his great love for her despite her age, not to mention
the amount of money she'd invested in an advertising campaign
emphasizing just those features . . ."

"Wait a minute! Wait a minute!" Trent shouted suddenly and
loudly. "I knew there was something if I could just think of what
it was, and now I've got it."

"I've got it too!" cried Melissa joyously. "Oh, Eric, Eric, isn't
it wonderful, wonderful?"

Carstairs woke up suddenly and stared at them in amazement.
They were dancing around like children at a Maypole.

"Well, I'll be a double-dyed Mexican blanket if I know what's
going on here," Doan said.

"Naturally," spoke up Sebastian Rodriguez y Ruiz, alias Morales, a worried and puzzled look on his dark face.

"Oh, you dopes!" Melissa taunted them. "Oh, you two big
stupid lumps who call yourselves detectives! It's perfectly obvious. Can't you see it? Why, Eric isn't married—isn't even a wid-
ower—hasn't been married at all. With Heloise married to Big
Tub, who wasn't dead like everybody thought, then her marriage
to Eric couldn't be legal. Oh, wonderful! Wonderful!"

"Yeah, yeah," said Doan. "I get that, but really the excitement—the cause for all this celebration . . . Well, really, it escapes me unless . . ." He stopped talking and smiled broadly.

"Not married," said Trent dazedly. "Think of that. A bachelor. Never married at all."

"Don't fret about it, darling," Melissa told him. "You soon will be . . . But go on, Doan. I forgive you for everything. I'll even go so far as to put your name back on my list."

Doan sighed a deep sigh and started all over again. "So Sebastian Rodriguez y Ruiz went to see Heloise and got himself played for a sucker. Then Heloise got rid of him and started figuring. She thought she could handle Big Tub. She had twenty servants and a gun, and she was tough. She called him up and told him she'd give him a twenty-four hour start or some kind of a start. She wanted to get rid of him without scandal. Big Tub started, all right—in her direction. She had lots of jewelry, and he needed some fast dough. He came in the back way and gathered up the servants—singly or in batches—and locked them away in the cellar. Then he interviewed her—with his gun. He must have been getting the shakes pretty badly by this time. He was playing in hellish luck. I don't think he heard you two arrive. About that time he was up in the back bedroom fiddling around in Heloise's wall safe. The first he knew about you was when the phone rang there's an extension in the bedroom. He heard you talking and hiked down and cut the wires and switched off the lights and locked the door on you and was waltzing out the front when he met me."

There was a sudden raging roar in the night, and Humphrey came billowing down the lawn toward them, pumping his legs furiously and waving his fists in the air.

"You!" he shouted. "As soon as I heard over the radio that there was some kind of a riot up here, I said to myself 'It's that damned Doan again,' and sure enough here you are! I've had enough of you! I've had all I'm going to take! What have you done to poor Professor Sley-Mynick? Look at, him lying there all wet and cold and unconscious, if not dead. Don't try to lie,

Doan. I warn you. You're under arrest right now!"

"Oh, relax," Doan advised. "I've just caught your murderer for you. He fell off the trellis, there, into the swimming pool and —"

"What?" Humphrey blurted. "Fell in the pool?" He ran to the edge and peered tensely in. "Where? Where?"

There was a sudden streak of fawn-colored shadow. A big body ran through Trent's legs and brushed past Melissa and made for Humphrey with the speed of a maddened goat, horns lowered, who's been waiting a long, long time for just the right opportunity.

"Carstairs!" Doan yelled frantically. "Don't you do it! Don't you dare. . ."

Humphrey shrieked and leaped right straight ahead, clutching his rear with both hands. The water swallowed him up with a cold and gleeful gulp.

"Carstairs!" Doan yelled. "You imbecile! You know he'll blame me for that! Do you want to see me in the gas chamber? Do you want to see me in jail for life?"

Carstairs ignored him. Carstairs was contemplating the frothy, turgid water in the pool with the remotely sadistic indifference of a scientist studying a pinned-down bug.

And Eric and Melissa ignored him too. For the moment they were too occupied with each other to have any interest in external affairs. Melissa's arms were about Eric's neck and he was holding her so closely that no biochemist or meteorologist or physicist or psychologist or any other scientist could have presented a logical explanation of how it was that she could breathe.

But she could, even though her lips were pressed close to his lips, and when their kiss was ended she sighed rapturously and long.

"Not married," Eric told her in a perfectly audible whisper. "Not married and never married to that old crow—God rest her. Now I have a right to ask you . . .Without any strings tied to it, I can offer you my name. You can be . . ."

"Stop! Stop!" Melissa cried, hugging him to her. "It's going to make you mad, maybe, but I can't help myself. I've just got to say it. It's too funny. If I don't say it I'll burst. . . Now I can be— can be *Mrs. Handsome Lover Boy!* There! I've done it! Don't strike me, Eric. . . Don't . . . Oh, oh! You aren't striking me . . . Oh, oh!"

"Naturally!" said Sebastian Rodriguez y Ruiz, alias Morales, watching the young couple go back into their clinch. "Naturally," he said again, and for the first time that evening smiled his broad Latin smile.

THE END

Carstairs and Doan appear in two previous books published by The Rue Morgue Press, *The Mouse in the Mountain* (0-915230-41-0) and *Sally's in the Alley* (0-915230-46-1).

The Rue Morgue has reprinted dozens of mysteries from the 1930s through the 1950s. For a catalog of publications or to suggest titles, write The Rue Morgue Press, P.O. Box 4119, Boulder, CO 80306.